No Place to Call Home

Book Two—The Eddie Brewster Adventures

By
Judith A. Schuster

Judith A. Schuster

PUBLISH AMERICA

PublishAmerica
Baltimore

*Jeremiah
29: 11-13*

Dedication

*This book is lovingly dedicated
to my husband,
Edwin Hiawatha Schuster,
whose stories of his unsettled childhood
became the basis for the fictional series:
The Eddie Brewster Adventures.*

Acknowledgments

I thank God for allowing many people to touch my life as I continue to write the *Eddie Brewster Adventures*. This list includes a few:

My appreciation to Louise B. Wyly, Professional Writing Consultant and my instructor at North Hennepin Community College in Brooklyn Park, MN.

Thanks to Edna Schuster, my husband's twin sister, for her support of this project and allowing me to base the fictional character "Ellie" on her life.

Thanks to Cindy Anderson and Sheryl Anne Lehman, Public Relations Representatives, for volunteering their time to assist in the marketing endeavors of *The Eddie Brewster Adventure Series*.

Thanks to four women who shared their foster care parenting experiences with me: Gretta Nelson, Betty Lundquist, Wendy Duske, and Carol Nelson. Our discussions helped me understand the resilience and determination it takes to be dedicated to the goal of giving quality foster care.

Thanks to Diane Bartz for discussing rabbit care with me, and allowing me to base the fictional character "Jessie" on her life.

Thanks to Lois and Robert Johnson of Buffalo, MN, for their encouragement and Robert's willingness to share his memories of life growing up on a farm in the 1940's-1950's.

Thanks to Rebecca Groos who gave me a tour of Minkota Holsteins, her family's farm in Howard Lake, MN, and for introducing me to their prizewinning herd of Holstein cows. During my tour, a brand new heifer calf, "Little Dipper," made her debut. What timing!

Thanks to the Potter's Clay Writer's Group of Buffalo, MN, for your helpful suggestions in manuscript reviews.

My deep gratitude is given to my family members for your love, support, and prayers that continually motivate me to write.

Glenwood City,
Wisconsin
August 1945

Chapter One

"Why can't she tell us where we're going?" I whispered to my twin sister Ellie as we rode to our next foster home. We sat in the back seat and I kicked my feet against the cardboard box that sat on the car floor. This was Ellie's box of clothes, a few books, and a small heart-shaped treasure box of girl's stuff.

"Stop that kicking back there," our social worker said in disgust. "Can't you just sit still and be quiet?"

I tried to hold my feet still, but they wanted to run. I began to bite my right thumb nail. I was about to burst. I wanted to know where our next home would be.

Ellie rubbed her eyes as silent tears leaked from her hurting heart. Only the hum of the car and Miss Westfield's red fingernails tapping on the steering wheel broke the silence.

I clutched the worn cardboard box in my lap. In it I had put my clothes and my baseball glove and ball. On top of these things, I laid the Bible story book from our first family, the Okerbys, and the Grand Champion ribbon that my calf Half-Pint won.

My old flashlight with dead batteries fit down on one side of the box. This was all that I owned in the world, except for a small chunk of thick green glass I secretly carried in my pant's pocket.

I touched my secret glass keepsake. I rolled it over a few times in my hand. It felt good to hold. It was mine. Over a year ago, I grabbed this "keeper" from an airplane crash that my foster brother Albert and I witnessed. Albert's father, a mean, irritable man, burned my Johnny Boy soldier, the only treasure I carried as a memory from my past. This time, I kept my treasure secretly hidden.

Why doesn't Miss Westfield say something? I feel like I have a lump in my throat as big as an orange. And my stomach hurts. We have a right to know where we're going.

For nine years we lived with the Okerbys. We always believed they were our own parents. They treated us like their children. Their photo albums held pages of dog-eared baby photos of us…even one picture of us eating our first birthday cake.

Then one summer day, when we were nine years old, a social worker visited. After she came, none of our childhood days mattered. We learned the family secret.

From that day on, everything changed…even our name. I was told my real name was "Eddie Brewster." A judge informed me that the Okerbys were not my own parents. He said my sister and I would have to leave their home. For two years we've been foster kids on the move. What surprises will we find in this next home?

Ellie lifted up her head and pushed her thick brown hair back from her face. I noticed her wet eyes were red from crying as she looked toward me for a moment.

I nudged my sister and asked her the big question.

"We have a right to know where we are going, Ellie. Should I ask her, again?" I whispered. Ellie shrugged her shoulders.

"Miss Westfield, we want to know where you're taking us," I said, as I felt a wave of bold anger wash over my heart.

"Humph. Childish impatience…and what can you do if it's not what you like?" Her scowling glare captured my eyes as she squinted and looked back in the rear view mirror. I watched her bright red lips accent each word as she mouthed another sarcastic answer. "I told you before, you'll get your answers soon enough. Nothing I say to you will change a thing."

The tears in my eyes welled up into pools of confusion. I tried to blink them away. I could see between the two front seats that Miss Westfield's open-toe red shoe pushed down extra hard on the accelerator. I figured she was in a big hurry to get us delivered to our new home. Then she'd be done with us. It wouldn't help to ask anymore questions.

I thought about the day we were taken away from Mother and Father Okerby. The pain cut like a knife. It was as if someone spilled ink over all the memories of our childhood. The welfare worker didn't give us enough time to say goodbye. And they didn't encourage us to see the Okerbys, even for a visit.

We've tried to think of a way to contact them again, but we couldn't come up with a plan. We missed their love and kindness. They were the only parents we knew, and we felt we belonged to them.

But now, after this move, I won't know how to reach them. They live in Hudson, but who knows where we're going? Mother Okerby said to us: "Remember, God is with you wherever you go, and He hears your prayers."

I've prayed many times the last two years. No one could please Mr. Schmidt. His anger would lash out when you'd least expect it. I know God helped us get through a lot of tough times in their home. I've prayed for God to find us another place to live. Is this move His answer to that prayer?

Chapter Two

I could see a small town just ahead as Miss Westfield reduced her speed. We approached a sign that read: GLENWOOD CITY.

Hey, I thought. That's the town where the county fair was held. But I don't remember traveling on this road when we went to the fair with the Schmidt family. We must have taken a different route when we were with them.

We drove through the town and then onto a dusty washboard road. A few more turns led us to a mailbox marked: FLETCHER FARM.

"You've arrived at your new home, children," Miss Westfield said crisply in her take-charge voice. "And we're right on schedule, too. Let's get your things and move along. Didn't I say you'd get your answers soon enough? By the way, you are the only kids that will be living in this house. The Fletchers do not have any children of their own."

I got out of the car and couldn't believe what I saw…a run-down farmhouse with a lawn that looked like it hadn't been mowed for weeks. An outdoor toilet with a door that sagged nearly off its hinges stood a short way behind the house.

Across the driveway, however, stood a well-kept white barn and other freshly painted out-buildings. But most amazing of all, behind the granary were railroad tracks running close to all the farm buildings. This should be interesting when a train comes chugging through.

"Come on, come on, don't just stand there looking around. Pick up your boxes and let's get to the house," Miss Westfield said, as she prodded us to walk faster through the tall grass leading up to the porch.

A fat green grasshopper popped up out of the weeds right in front of her face. She jumped off the overgrown path for a moment. "What a mess this lawn is," she fussed. "Oh, drat! I've picked up burrs in my silk stockings. I should have worn different shoes for this trip into the wilderness."

Another grasshopper jumped up and landed on Ellie's sleeve. She smiled... Then it bolted to my shoulder. I caught the little creature and dropped him back into his home in the weeds.

As we climbed the porch steps, the top stair creaked and gave way so that Miss Westfield lost her balance. She grabbed the railing for support, but in the process, her thick lens, dark-rimmed glasses sailed into the air and landed in the middle of a bed of faded pink hollyhocks at the side of the porch.

"O, for crying out loud!" she fussed as she reached down where the rough prickly burrs grew amongst the tall withering hollyhock stems. She fumbled clumsily to find her glasses. "There's no excuse for this! I could have broken my ankle.

"Ouch! These burrs are sharp. Where did my glasses land?" she asked, as she patted the ground wildly. "I can't see a thing. Children, get down here right now and help me find them."

In a moment's relief from our sadness, we both tried hard not to giggle. Miss Westfield was down on all fours, prickle burrs in her silk stockings, and dirt on her fancy, red, high-heeled shoes. The lady who didn't want to answer our questions now wanted us to answer hers.

"Miss Westfield, I think your glasses are in the dirt next to your skirt," I said trying hard to be serious.

"Oh, yes. Here they are," she said as she stood up and brushed the dust off her navy blue skirt. I'll certainly make a note of this broken step. It is a dreadful safety hazard. It must be repaired immediately."

She knocked loudly on the fly-speckled screen door. We kids waited on the ground next to the rickety stairway. She dusted off her glasses on the sleeve of her blouse.

She knocked once again and called: "Hello there...is anyone home?"

I listened and heard a rocking sound that seemed to come from inside the house. Miss Westfield knocked again. The noise stopped. I noticed a face peek out at us from behind the lace curtain in the window to our right. A pale looking woman with uncombed hair came to the door in a grungy, gray bathrobe. "Oh, I didn't hear you drive up. I was rocking the baby. I'm Mary Fletcher," she extended a thin hand to Miss Westfield.

"Ah, yes..." our social worker said with a sour look. "This is Eddie and Ellie Brewster, your foster children. They have their belongings in these boxes. I'm going to be on my way. But first, I need you to sign this sheet that says I have brought them here. Will you do that?"

"Yes, where shall I sign?" Mrs. Fletcher said with a vacant look.

"Right on this line, please," she said. "Thank you. I want you to know that I'm making a note of this safety hazard. You'll want to get this step repaired. I almost fell. It is extremely dangerous."

"Oh, yes. There are a lot of projects that need doing on a farm," Mrs. Fletcher said in a weak voice. "I'm not a lot of help now with the baby and all the work there is."

I looked at Ellie and she looked at me. Neither of us said what we were thinking. *A baby?* This woman keeps talking about *a baby.* Miss Westfield said this couple didn't have children. She sighed and shook her head as she scanned the step, the long grass, and the entire poorly cared for farm. Without any further word to us, she walked down the weedy path, climbed into her black sedan, and drove off down the gravel road in a cloud of dust.

Mary Fletcher smiled at us. "Come in, children, we've been waiting for you. This is the first day of your stay at Fletcher Farm, and as you can see, we really need your help around here."

Chapter Three

My first step into this old farm kitchen made me want to walk back outside. Mrs. Fletcher certainly needed help. Dirty dishes filled the table. The sideboard held pots and pans stacked up from several meals. Flies darted here and there, sitting on bowls of food that needed to be thrown out. An odor of spoiled garbage came from an overflowing garbage can near the cupboard. I glanced at Ellie for a moment. She looked overwhelmed.

If she figured she had a lot of clean-up to do at the Schmidt's, I could just about guess what she was thinking now.

"I know this place is a mess," Mary Fletcher said pushing her hair back from her face. "I planned to get going on it before you got here, but the baby has been fussy."

Mrs. Fletcher wandered into the large living room and adjusted her grubby looking bathrobe. I whispered, "Ellie, what is going on here?"

She shrugged her shoulders and said softly, "This place is strange."

We followed our foster mother into the living room. This room smelled musty. I wanted to plug my nose. The burgundy couch with scrolled arms stood on the wall under the front window. A stained gold chair sat on the opposite wall next to a table and floor lamp.

I spotted a wind-up victrola in the corner next to a shelf of records. Facing the kitchen sat a rocking chair. Its arms were worn smooth. On the floor lay a large rug with raveled worn spots.

"Children," Mrs. Fletcher said, "Come with me and I'll show you where your bedrooms are." She led us up the oak stairway off one side of the living room.

With a fearful look in her eyes, she pointed to the room at the top of the stairs. "This room is restricted to both of you. No one may enter here, but me. Do you understand?"

We nodded yes, but said nothing aloud. The tone in her voice was stressful, but it didn't compare to the wave of despair that washed over her face.

"If I can't trust you to follow this rule," she said as she pushed her hair back, "you can't live in this house. Is that clear? You are not to speak of this room to anyone else, and by all means, never go inside."

I swallowed hard. Here is another adult trying to hide a piece of truth. What was behind that door? What didn't she want us to know? Now we're victims caught up in her secret, too. A strange world that we don't know anything about lay behind that door.

"You can each take one of the other rooms," she told us pointing down the hall. "Go ahead and unpack your boxes and then come downstairs. We'll see if we can get the kitchen cleaned up before my husband gets back from the cattle sale. He will have plenty for you to do in the barn, Eddie, so we can use your help until he gets home. Let's hope the baby takes a good long nap this afternoon." She turned and sloshed down the creaking stairs in her bedroom slippers, clutching her robe around her.

"I'll take this pink room," Ellie said." "I'd like to be as far away from her mystery room as possible."

"Thanks," I said sarcastically. "Oh well, I guess I'll be brave and take the other one since it's my only choice. Both rooms smell. They look like they need a good clean up."

My room was a beige color with plaster cracks on every wall. The windows were not large. They did let in some daylight, and they gave me a view of the backyard. A dirty lace curtain hung limply at my window creating a frame for a delicate spider web. The weaver created a masterpiece of perfect balance. His design reached across the entire upper glass pane. I left it for the moment.

An outdated calendar from 1943 hung on one wall. It advertised the Farmington Mutual Insurance Company in Osceola, Wisconsin. The page was stuck at the month of June of that year. I thought back to that time of my life... I was still living with Mother and Father Okerby. I didn't know the "family secret" or realize what was about to happen to us. Now Ellie and I have moved again, still further from the Okerby family. Will we ever find them?

In each of our rooms stood a dresser and a single bed with a thin, stained, old mattress. On the end of the bed in Ellie's room, someone had laid out two pillows, two blankets, and some mismatched sheets and pillowcases.

"Here are some sheets for your bed," Ellie said, as she handed me an armful of bedding. "And here's your pillow."

"This pillow stinks," I said. "It smells like someone just took it out of a damp basement."

"Mine does too," Ellie said. "Just put your pillow case on it and let's hope the smell will eventually go away."

"Ellie, what about this 'baby' Mrs. Fletcher talks about?" I asked. "The next time she mentions it, I'm going to ask her: *what baby?* I'm sick of this secret stuff...and now a room we can't enter. Isn't that really strange?"

"I know, we haven't seen a baby since we walked in the front door, and the social worker said there were no other kids in this family. What could she be talking about?"

"Who knows?"

We finished our beds, and then we went downstairs. We met our foster mom back in the kitchen. She was wearing a blue cotton print housedress. Her brown shoulder length hair was brushed back away from her face. She had put on a red and white checked apron, but she stood waiting for us to help her begin the clean up work.

"We'd best be getting going. It's nearly lunchtime," Mrs. Fletcher said. "Eddie, you can get us a fire going in the cook stove so we can heat some dish water. The wood box in the kitchen is nearly out of wood. There's more out on the back porch. Pump some water into this big kettle and set it to heating.

"Ellie, you and I will move these dishes to organize a work area. It's going to be great having some help around here…what with the baby being fussy and all."

"Mrs. Fletcher, what baby are you talking about?" I asked as I shoved the pieces of wood into the cook stove. From my comment, she turned to me and hurled an answer I was unprepared for.

"Listen to me, young man," she snapped. The calm expression on her face disappeared. In a voice of alarm she continued: "I don't take to sarcastic kids or having to explain everything. You just mind what I say and we'll get along fine."

Our foster mother's speech ended when we heard someone pull up in the driveway. A tall, slender man walked into the kitchen. He wore overalls and a denim shirt with rolled up sleeves. He took off his western hat revealing his thick brown hair, and he wiped his brow with his red handkerchief.

"Hello there, kids. I'm Russell Fletcher. Welcome to Fletcher Farm," he said with a grin, as he hung his hat on the hat rack.

"Hi," we answered.

"I want you to know you're going to have the privilege of

working with the best herd of Holsteins around," he said, looking directly at me. His dark brown eyes shown as he talked about his herd.

"This will be a great opportunity for you, Eddie. I've needed a good right-hand man to help with my cattle."

I noticed that as he spoke, he did not direct one word of conversation toward his wife, nor did she speak to him.

"On this farm the cows come first. We produce quality milk because we give our cattle quality care, the best feed, the cleanest barn, and spotless milking equipment. Nothing but the best…and the milk reports prove it! Grade A Milk is what we produce from our Holstein herd."

As Mr. Fletcher continued, I could feel the enthusiasm in his voice. This was a farm and herd he was proud of. He would work hard and sacrifice most anything for it.

The water began to heat and our foster mother slowly filled the dishpan in the sink. Ellie got started washing the pile of dirty dishes. However, she seemed left alone to face this miserable task as Mrs. Fletcher wandered out of the kitchen. I watched her walk into the living room and start up the stairs. Then I heard the door at the top of the stairs close. Ellie looked at me. I could see the frustration sweep over her face. Would Mrs. Fletcher come back to help?

"You come with me, Eddie. We've got men's work to do outside," Mr. Fletcher said. "I want to show you around."

Chapter Four

"Just want you to know you're standing on Fletcher Farmland that's been in the family for a hundred and fifty years. My granddaddy first worked this soil with my daddy, and then he deeded it to me in his will. I'm his only son and he knew I could do a right good job farming it. Yep, I own one-hundred and sixty acres here."

"Why does the railroad track run through the middle of the farm like that?" I asked. "Isn't it a big nuisance to have a train come through here so close to everything you're trying to do?"

"Well, you could look at it that way, I suppose. But the railroad sends me a nice check that sweetens the inconvenience. That money helps me pay for other things I need. I own land on both sides of the track and I pasture my cattle across the tracks way down in the rich pastureland. I simply am aware of the train schedule and I move the cattle across and secure them into the pasture on the other side, where they stay until I move them back for evening milking."

"I guess that would work," I said.

"I'm glad you do, because it will be your job to get the cattle across the tracks to pasture after the morning's milking, and then back home again in the late afternoon. You have to know the train schedule and allow yourself enough time to accomplish the job. There's a copy of the schedule hanging in the milk house."

Wow, that could get to be a bit tricky, I thought. What if a cow strayed off onto the track? I'd be in big trouble!

"How many milk cows do you have?" I asked as we walked toward the barn.

"I milk thirty of the best looking Holstein cows you've ever laid eyes on," he said. "You're going to love working with them. I don't raise pigs, or chickens, or anything else. Just my fine herd of Holsteins...but they're my pride and joy."

This barn was the cleanest building around. The whole interior was white-washed. It didn't even smell like cow manure. I couldn't believe it. This made me miss my 4-H calf Half-Pint. I wondered where he was now. I hoped he was living in someone's nice clean barn. I noticed some kittens running and playing on a bale of hay. A calico mother cat was busy cleaning her paws.

"You'll notice, we lime the gutters...keeps them fresh...it adds to a good clean environment for our cows. We treat them right, and they produce high quality milk for us. The best there is, in fact."

"I have another question," I ventured. "This one is not about your herd."

"Well, go ahead. Speak up."

"When the social worker brought us over, she said you didn't have children. Since we've arrived, Mrs. Fletcher's been talking about a baby. Who's she talking about?"

"We lost a baby over a year ago. My wife never got over the sorrow of our loss. The doctor did surgery at that time. He told us she could never have another baby. Since that time, she's become depressed. Now her depression has taken over her life.

"There are times when she does not even wish to speak to me. She just sits and stares. She will not eat her meals, and she refuses to do any activity inside or outside on our farm. She says she hears a voice of a baby crying, and then she sits holding a rolled up towel in the rocking chair. It nearly drives me crazy. The baby is dead. We can't change that. We have to move on," Mr. Fletcher said as he bowed his head and wiped a tear from his eye.

"I'm sorry your baby died," I said softly.

"Sometimes at night she roams about the house. She can't sleep. She sees things that aren't there and hears voices I can't hear. If I tell her to go back to bed, she becomes angry. She says things that don't make sense. She made me move the crib and all the things we had ready for our baby into that room upstairs, and she won't let me or anyone else go in there. She's a sick woman. But the doctor thinks perhaps in time her strange mental state will run its course and she will come back to her old self.

"If you ask me, I doubt it. She lives in her own world, and I think she's gone too far. They have hospitals for people like that...people who can't get control of life.

"I go outside and work and leave her alone. She doesn't want me around anyway. There's not much left of our marriage. She always hated this farm, so that only makes it worse. She never wanted to move here from the city."

"Does she have any friends or neighbors she can talk to since she moved to the farm?" I asked. "Maybe she's lonesome and needs a friend."

"She knows our neighbors by their names, but she didn't want to get together to visit with them like some neighbors do. She used to work at a fancy dress shop in Hudson, and she had girlfriends when she lived there. But she stopped seeing them when she married me and moved out on our farm."

"That's too bad."

"I guess she never got over wanting pretty clothes, and the nice things that you can have when you have money and live in the city. But living on the farm isn't like that. She might have been depressed even before she had the baby.

"She always wants to spend money to fix up the house. But I say we got to take care of the barn first because the cows are our livelihood. If we don't take care of the cows, we don't have a good milk check. That's just how it is…plain and simple.

"The doctor thinks maybe you foster kids might help us out. Your sister can help her with the work and cheer her up. If its kids she wants, she can look after you twins."

As I heard Mr. Fletcher talk, I wasn't convinced that we would be the cure-all for our foster mom's problems. At least now I could tell Ellie that Mrs. Fletcher used to live in Hudson…that's the first connection with that city I've heard about since we left Mother and Father Okerby's.

"I'll be back in a bit, Mr. Fletcher," I said. "I'm going to the outhouse."

"Okay. I'll put fresh bedding in the calves' pen, and then we'll get some lunch."

Spiders and bugs of all kinds lived in the Fletcher's outdoor toilet. Mice chewed the corners of the Sears and Roebuck catalog that we used for toilet paper. The sagging door allowed most any creature to come and go at will. As I sat down, I felt something move behind my foot. Out from behind a loose board slithered a swift wriggling garter snake. It gave me a start, but he hurried on his way as fast as he appeared. I decided not to tell Ellie about the snake. She would be horrified. I hoped it was his one and only visit to this outdoor bathroom.

Chapter Five

As my tour of the out-buildings with Mr. Fletcher ended, we came up to the house for lunch. The stinking pail of garbage now sat on the porch. As we entered the house, Ellie stood alone in the kitchen. She looked irritated as she wiped the last few dishes.

"Has the missus been in here to help you at all?" Richard Fletcher asked.

"Nope, she hasn't," Ellie answered sharply. "She's been singing lullabies in the upstairs room."

Mr. Fletcher's angry face gave way to exasperation as he paused a moment to listen.

"Well, if that doesn't beat all," he said. "I figured she'd at least try when you kids moved here. I'm going to talk to her about this."

His heavy brown work shoes repeated a defiant thump with every step up the stairs to the mysterious room.

He knocked determinedly. "Mary, are you listening to me?" his voice booming loud enough for us to hear from the kitchen.

We could hear her singing stop.

"Mary, answer me. The children are hungry and you need to fix lunch. Are you coming downstairs?"

We heard nothing.

"Mary, remember we talked about this when the doctor suggested it might be good for you to have these children in our house? You said you would try. They can't stay, Mary, if you don't try. Mary, are you listening to me?"

Once again, our foster mother chose not to answer her husband's questions, and then we heard his loud footsteps come back down the stairway.

"Let's eat some sandwiches, kids," Mr. Fletcher said, as he joined us. He went to the cupboard and pulled out a loaf of bread, some peanut butter, and the cookie jar. "We've got apples, too," he said, as he brought out a basket of bright red fruit from another cupboard. He reached into the icebox for a pitcher of milk.

Ellie put some clean plates and silverware on the table, and I grabbed three glasses and filled them with cold milk.

As Mr. Fletcher busied himself pulling the items from the shelves, I noticed a swift brown mouse scurry from the lower cupboard, run right behind his feet, and hurry along the sideboard. It bolted quickly under the kitchen cook stove. The little thing moved so fast, I was taken by surprise. I didn't want to upset Ellie, so I didn't say anything to Mr. Fletcher about this four-legged creature.

We sat down at the table which was covered with a worn, faded, red plaid oilcloth. If what Mr. Fletcher said was true, I suppose the neglected state of things around this farmhouse could add to his wife's discouragement. If she was used to spending her earnings on beautiful things, then the broken back step and this old oilcloth on her table, and a mouse in her kitchen might be a difficult adjustment from her city lifestyle.

"I don't know what to do with her," Mr. Fletcher said. "I'm not sure Doc Robards does either. I think he's holding off putting her in the hospital so we can say we tried everything else first. She won't take her medicine, and now I see she's not cooperating with you kids. I'm ready to send her to the hospital right now. It's the only answer that I can see. "

We heard footsteps on the stairway and turned to see Mary Fletcher walking toward the kitchen. She carried a rolled up towel as if it were an infant.

"I'm sorry I left you, Ellie," she said, "but when the baby needs me, I must go to her."

"Now Mary, you know that's just not so," Mr. Fletcher said. "Put that towel down and have some lunch. I made a sandwich for you," Mr. Fletcher said with a scowl.

I got another glass and poured some milk for Mrs. Fletcher as she sat down at the table.

"Mary, Mrs. Benson is coming over this afternoon to help you do the wash. We have lots of dirty clothes. Ellie will help you, too. You can hang the clothes on the line. It's a nice day. They'll dry fast. Mary, are you listening to me? I wish you would look at me when I talk to you," he said angrily as he hit the table with his fist.

His wife made no comment, nor did she even look at him. She began to rock the rolled up towel gently in her arms, again.

I looked at Ellie and she frowned at me. A shrug of her shoulders communicated my thoughts exactly: What kind of a situation have we gotten into now?

Chapter Six

"Eddie, we're going over to pick up the calves I bought at the sale I went to this morning," Mr. Fletcher said. "I'm anxious for you to meet the cattle buyer and see his herd. He's got some fine stock."

"That sounds great to me," I said as we cleared our dishes off the table. It was a hundred times better than cleaning eggs for Mr. Schmidt, I thought. I grabbed my hat and followed Mr. Fletcher outside.

"I'm going to throw this garbage in the manure spreader before we leave," Mr. Fletcher said. "We can rinse the pail out in the barn and then bring it back up to the house."

"I'll run it back to the house," I said. I felt anxious to get on our way to the sale barn.

We climbed into his pick-up with the trailer securely hitched behind. The gravel roads were bumpy and a cloud of dust followed us all the way to the sale barn.

"This cattle buyer picks up fine stock wherever he sees them," Mr. Fletcher said. "He bought some good calves at the county fair here in Glenwood City."

My heart skipped a beat. Do you suppose it would be the same buyer that bought Half-Pint? It would be incredible if I could see my 4-H calf again. I decided not to say anything. I'd just wait and see who this guy was.

I'd never forget what he looked like…large western hat, cowboy boots, that toothpick always floating about in his mouth as he spoke…and the slow smile peeking out from behind his large moustache. No, I'd never forget the pain of leaving Half-Pint, my obedient 4-H calf with the likes of this cattle jockey…nice as he might be.

A few more miles and we came to a mailbox and a sign that read: **GRANGER FARMS—Cattle-Bought and Sold**

"I bought three good looking heifer calves," Mr. Fletcher said, as he turned into the driveway leading up to the large cattle barns on this impressive looking property.

"Well, here's the farm, Eddie."

I hopped out of the truck and surveyed the scene. A young man, who looked a few years older than me walked up. He pushed his cowboy hat up on his forehead. Trickles of sweat trailed through the dust on his face. He smiled and said: "I'm Larry Granger, can I help you folks?"

"Yes, Sir… I'm Richard Fletcher and I'm here to pick up the three heifer calves I bought at the sale this morning. This is Eddie Brewster. He lives at my house."

The young man nodded and continued, "Bring your trailer down to that far gate and we'll get you loaded. I'll tell my dad you're here."

As Mr. Fletcher backed the truck and trailer down to the gate, I stood by the fence and looked at the calves in that pen. Within a few minutes, a tall, thin man in cowboy boots and a western hat came up to the gate where I stood. A slow smile inched out from behind his large moustache and I noticed a toothpick in the corner of his mouth.

"Say, haven't we met somewhere before?" he asked, as he extended his right hand. "I'm Will Granger, if you don't remember. I believe you lived with Otto Schmidt, didn't you? Over near Roberts?"

"Yes, I did. Now I'm living with the Fletchers," I said, as I shook the man's hand. "My name's Eddie Brewster."

"That's right. I remembered because of the fine calf you raised. I bought him from Schmidt, but I'm keeping that calf as a sire for my herd. He's not for sale. Would you like to see him?" Mr. Granger asked.

"I sure would," I said.

I felt a grin wash over my face and my heart began to pound like a drum. Never in the world did I think I would see my Half-Pint again. Was this really happening? To me?

Will Granger led me into his ultra-clean barn. There stood Half-Pint in a fresh, straw-bedded stall of his own. What a nice life for my grand-prize winner.

"Hello there my buddy, you're looking great! I'm glad you've got a fine place to live. And you've gained weight, too," I said as I scratched his soft ears. He looked at me as if to say "*Where in the world have you been?*"

"Yes, he's grown all right, and he has a great disposition," Mr. Granger said. "You trained him well."

A bit later, Richard Fletcher's voice caught me off guard. "Oh, here you are, Eddie."

"This used to be my 4-H calf, Half-Pint. I raised him from a sickly, scrawny calf that Mr. Schmidt was going to put down," I said proudly. "Mr. Schmidt let me try to work with him and Half-Pint fought to live. He made it! I entered him at the fair, where he won a grand champion, purple ribbon. Mr. Granger saw him and bought him for his herd. And now look at him! Isn't he handsome!"

I grinned at Half-Pint as he continued to chew the fresh hay in his feed box. "I couldn't be happier that he has such a great place to live," I told Mr. Granger. Tucked back in my mind, I remembered praying for that sickly little calf. I prayed God would let him live so I could learn to care for him and train him. That calf was my little buddy, and God answered my prayer. On top of that, I got to see him here—another answer to my prayers.

"Well Eddie, we'd better be getting on home," Richard Fletcher said. "We're loaded and ready to go."

I gave Half-Pint one more pat on the head, then I left the barn with Mr. Fletcher. I thanked God once more for letting me see my buddy again.

Chapter Seven

As we pulled up into the Fletcher's driveway, I could see clothes flapping in the breeze. "Hi Ellie," I said, as I entered the kitchen. I walked to the sink to pump myself a glass of water.

"You'll never believe who I got to see over at the sale barn..."

"Who did you see?" she asked as she checked our supper in the oven.

"I saw Half-Pint and his new owner, Mr. Granger," I answered.

"Eddie, you mean it? Your own calf?" Ellie shouted with joy.

"Well, he's not mine anymore, but he lives like a king in a large, clean stall with plenty of fresh water and good food. He is calm and well behaved as always. I got to scratch his ears and He loved it. It was great to see him again. Mr. Granger is keeping him to sire his prize herd."

"I'm so glad you got to see him again," Ellie said. "If he would have gone back to the Schmidt farm, he would be meat on their table by now."

Mr. Fletcher came into the house. "Did Mrs. Benson come and help the missus with the wash?" he asked.

"Mrs. Benson and I did the wash, and then we made some supper and put it in the oven. Mrs. Fletcher is upstairs in her room again," Ellie said.

"I can't believe it. That really beats all," Richard Fletcher said, as he slapped his brown, sweat-stained western hat down on the table in frustration. "That woman isn't trying one bit to help you kids.

"We need to see some progress here. Your new school will start in two weeks. Doc Robards wants answers, and the welfare wants answers, too.

"Let her sit up there in that room then. You kids come with me," Mr. Fletcher said. "We've got enough time before supper and milking so that I can drive you by the school you'll be attending."

Suddenly, our conversation was interrupted. The ground began to rumble, and the dishes in the cupboard rattled. The four o'clock train came pounding through. Now I realized how close this train actually came to the granary and the other buildings on the farm.

Crash! "Oh, no…there goes our picture of 'The Gleaners,'" Richard Fletcher said. "My mama hung it up there above the side board, and we've never moved it. It gets to swinging back and forth when the train goes by, but sometimes it gets loose enough to fall on the floor. The glass broke long ago and we've never replaced it." He picked up the old family antique and set it on its nail again.

"The trains that come through here cause a mean vibration, that's for sure."

After the train went by, we climbed into the pick-up with Mr. Fletcher. I was anxious to see our new school.

"You'll have about a mile to walk, but the road is good. In case of a snowstorm, the plow comes through first thing. They have to keep the road open for the milk truck."

We approached the small one-room school house. It reminded me of the last school we attended. I hoped I would make new friends in this place. I could feel that empty pain starting in my stomach again...that awful sinking sense of starting over in a different school. I hated it.

I looked at Ellie. She bit her lip and was about to cry. I wondered if she was thinking the same thoughts I was.

"How many kids go to school in this building?" I asked.

"When I went to school here, we had about thirty students. But that's a long time ago. I'm not sure how many kids attend here now.

"My sister, Joanne and I went from first through sixth grade in this old building. Joanne always loved book-learning, and now she's a teacher in Green Bay. I'm right proud of her. Don't get to see her much, though... Both our parents are dead, so she doesn't come back here often..."

Mr. Fletcher's voice trailed off as he backed out of the school yard and headed his pick-up toward home.

"Ellie, ask Mary to help you get supper on the table," he continued.

I saw Ellie nod and push her long brown hair back as she went into the house. I had a feeling it would be Ellie that would put our supper on the table. Who could count on Mrs. Fletcher to help with anything?

"Eddie, you can help me get the cows across the tracks from the meadow. We'll get the cows in the barn and feed them. Then we'll come up and eat."

"Okay," I said.

We walked off toward the fence that ran along the railroad track.

"This system works as long as we follow the schedule. It's important that we don't move any cattle around four o'clock. People used to call that contraption on the front of the steam engines a *cow catcher*. However, we don't want to literally prove that we can catch cows with the engines that go by here."

"How do you get them to follow along where they're supposed to go?" I asked. "Don't any of them run off on their own?"

"The key is to open the gate in the direction you're going first, and have the herd set to go. Always make sure you have Susie in the lead. She's the cow that's been doing this the longest. Get her going in the right direction, and the others will come along behind her.

"They want to get into the barn at night for their grain and milking so they're willing to move right along. We'll do it together so you can get the hang of it."

Just at that moment, Ellie came running down to the fence. "Mr. Fletcher, I think you need to see this." Ellie handed our foster father a note.

"No, I can't believe this." Richard Fletcher groaned, and a worried look flooded his face.

Chapter Eight

"Kids, it seems Mary has decided to leave us. Listen to this note from Mrs. Benson: "*Hi Richard: I saw Mary walking on the road past our farm with a suitcase and something that looked like a rolled up towel in her arm. I tried to call out to her, but she ignored me and kept on walking. I came over to tell you, but no one was home. I'm leaving this note because I am very worried about Mary. It seems to me she is seriously in need of help. Let me know if I can do anything. Leona Benson*"

"She's gone on walks before...but never with a suitcase," he said. "I just can't go look for her until the cows are milked," Richard Fletcher added. "I'll call Doc Robards and the police, and they can be on the lookout for her. I'll go in after milking and join the search.

"Eddie, stay with the cattle," Mr. Fletcher said, as he turned to me with a worried look. "I'll make these phone calls and be right back."

"Okay," I said. I watched him stride toward the house with my sister.

He returned quickly. He looked like he carried the weight of the world on his shoulders.

"Eddie, you circle behind the herd and move them along. Susie is coming up front here already. She knows it's milking time and wants to get to the barn for her grain. The others will come. Just call to them," Mr. Fletcher said.

"Come, girl," I called. "Move along now," I said as I walked between the cows. "Come, girl. Let's go."

I noticed when one decided to move along, it encouraged another to go, and another, and soon the herd realized what the plan was. It meant food and milking time ahead, and seeing Susie lead out, they all decided to follow.

I watched the cows go into their stanchions to enjoy their feed. Now it was our turn to go up to the house for our supper.

The aroma of a wonderful oven meal that Mrs. Benson and Ellie made welcomed us as we walked through the door. We hung up our hats and washed up for supper.

We sat down at the table and began eating the tasty beef roast, potatoes, and carrots. After eating a few bites, Mr. Fletcher put down his fork and left the table. He walked upstairs. We heard him force open the door to the forbidden room.

"Oh no!" we heard him. "That woman is crazy!"

After a few minutes he clomped back down the stairs, his chin clenched rigidly in a wave of agony.

"She's torn apart everything in those dresser drawers. The baby clothes, toys, sheets, blankets, everything we had for our little one. Everything is heaped together in a big pile on the floor. What would she do a thing like that for?"

I could see the pain in Mr. Fletcher's eyes…pain for the loss of his child, but also pain for the loss of his wife suffering from her strange behavior.

"When you're done eating, Eddie," Mr. Fletcher said grabbing his hat, "we'll do the milking. Then I'll get into town and talk to the doctor to get her the kind of help she needs."

He stopped and turned back to Ellie. "Thanks for a good supper, Ellie. Sorry all you've had to do is work since you came here. Now we can't help you clean up the supper mess, either." He shook his head, plopped on his hat, turned and walked out the door.

I looked at Ellie and saw her nod. She sighed deeply at the prospect of being the only person in the house to manage the inside chores.

"At least we're not living with Mr. Schmidt," I reminded her. "I'll see you later." I grabbed my cap and went to the barn to help milk the cows.

* * *

Thankfully, the milking went smoothly. We hauled the cans of fresh milk into the water cooler. After we turned the cows back out to the pasture for the night, Mr. Fletcher left for town to join the authorities searching for his wife. I continued shoveling the manure and any mud from the cow's hooves into the gutter. Then I spread fresh lime onto the surfaces.

I heard the rumble of the evening freight...the Nine O' Five as Mr. Fletcher called it, was steadily approaching from down the track. I continued to work, but as the train went by, I looked up... There in the dusk, I saw a shadow leap wildly from the train into the long grass near the tracks. Was I seeing things?

Chapter Nine

"What?" I said to myself. "Did I imagine this, or is someone out there?" I finished up in the barn and began searching in the brush by the tracks and around the buildings.

Maybe a person could hide in one of the smaller sheds, or even crawl up into the hay mow, I thought. I saw nothing suspicious in either the machine shed or the small tool shed, so I headed back toward the barn.

"Hey, is anyone up there?" I shouted, as I inched myself halfway up the hay mow ladder.

"Yah, kid. Come up here. I need to talk to you."

It wasn't my imagination after all. I'd heard people talk about bums that rode the freight trains when I lived at the Okerbys. *"You could never trust a stranger,"* they had said. Yet it seemed to me everyone I met in the last two years had been strangers. How did I know what any of them would do, or if they could be trusted?

I knew what I had been told, and yet I had a funny feeling about this guy. His voice sounded like he needed help. What if he got hurt when he jumped from the train? I decided to take a risk and check it out.

"What's the matter?" I asked as my heart began to pound.

In the dim barn light I could see this stranger looked rough. He wasn't a big man, and when I looked into his eyes, I didn't feel afraid.

"I'm hungry and I need a drink of water," he said. He was dressed in dirty, old bib-overalls and wore a faded engineer cap. Strands of his dark hair were matted against his forehead.

"I'll get you something, but you'd better stay up there. What's wrong with your arm?" I could see blood oozing through his torn blue-denim shirt, and then soaking into his left sleeve.

"I scraped it good when I jumped the train," he said, as he held his arm close to his left side.

"I'll be back with some food and water for you."

I climbed down the ladder to get him some supper. I decided not to breathe a word to Ellie about this mysterious looking guy. She would not feel safe about me talking to a stranger neither of us knew.

Ellie was up in her room, so it was easy for me to make a couple roast beef sandwiches. I grabbed an empty cream bucket and filled it with cold water for our visitor to enjoy with his supper. I found an old towel to wrap around his arm, and then I ran down to the barn and climbed up into the hay mow.

"Food tastes mighty good when you're on the run," the stranger said. I wanted to offer him a place to clean up, but I wasn't sure what being *on the run* meant. Richard Fletcher might not look kindly on a stranger cleaning up in his milk house if the stranger was a runaway from the law.

"Say kid, what's your name?"

"Eddie Brewster."

"I figured. You got a twin sister staying here, too?"

"Yes, I do. How did you know?"

"Just been doing some checking."

I looked at this man and something about him made me feel like I had known him before. Was it his eyes? The curve of his whiskery chin?

I wrapped the towel around his left arm to absorb some of the blood. He patted my shoulder with his big right hand.

"Thanks. You don't know what you've done for me tonight. You're a fine lad. I want you to have this. It's a leather watch fob. This attaches to a pocket watch. And see, it has my initials O. B. carved in the leather.

"I had to trade my watch for food, so I can't use the watch fob now. Maybe someday you'll get a watch, and then you can use the fob and think of me. You've been a good friend to me. I really appreciate meeting you. Remember to take care of that sister of yours."

"Okay, I'll bring you some breakfast in the morning," I said as I climbed down the hay mow ladder. I thought he mumbled something else, but he seemed so tired I just let him go to sleep and didn't ask him any more questions.

I wonder who this guy is, I thought. How does he know so much about us? Why do I feel like I've seen him before?

As I started toward the house, Ellie met me. "Why were you down in the barn so long?" she asked.

Before I could answer, Mr. Fletcher drove in the driveway. "Hi kids," he said. "Come up to the house. We have lots to talk about."

We pulled our chairs around the kitchen table as Mr. Fletcher began to speak.

"My wife has been found and taken to the local hospital for tonight. Tomorrow Doc Robards will admit her to the State Hospital for psychological evaluation and treatment. She won't be coming back here to live until their medical staff feels she is well enough to handle life.

"This means that within a day or two a social worker will come and take you each to a different home."

"What do you mean?" Ellie asked. "Each one of us to a *different* home?"

"The home in St. Croix County that the welfare has chosen for

Eddie has room for only one child because they already have eight children of their own," Mr. Fletcher said.

"I'm not moving away from my brother," Ellie cried. "I'll run away first."

I couldn't believe this was happening. To be a foster kid was one thing, but seeing my sister move away from me was something I hadn't thought would happen. It seemed unbearable.

"I've tried, kids," Mr. Fletcher said. "Believe me, I've tried to keep you here. I know we could have made a good home for you both. But the welfare won't let you stay without a foster mother. They warned us about that before you came."

Ellie was still crying. She held her head in her hands and sobbed quietly. In our other moves, we were never separated. We always had each other. How could the welfare do such a thing?

I moved my chair closer and patted her shoulder. She rocked back and forth with heavy pain silently crushing her heart. I had never felt so helpless. We kids were like checkers on a checker board, moved about at the whim of another stranger. Wasn't there anything we could do?

Chapter Ten

We sat around the kitchen table quietly trying to eat our ham sandwiches. But how could we eat after hearing the dreadful news that Mr. Fletcher laid on us last night? Now the awful facts had begun to sink in for both of us.

I noticed Ellie's eyes were puffed and red and my own unwept tears were beginning to give me a headache. I had envisioned working with Mr. Fletcher and his great herd of Holsteins for a long time. Now that dream was gone, too. I could see no purpose for small talk when our lives were about to be torn apart once more.

The phone rang, and Mr. Fletcher answered it. "Hello, yes Mrs. Johnson, This is Richard Fletcher. This afternoon? Already?"

My sandwich lumped in my throat. Was this our social worker? Was she coming today? Is that what this conversation was about? And who were they coming to take? Would it be me first? I felt the pressure begin to build. I didn't eat the rest of my lunch.

"Well Ellie," Mr. Fletcher said. "Your social worker will be here in about two hours. Let's leave the dishes and we'll all help you get your things packed."

Later that afternoon, a black sedan came driving up the Fletcher's driveway. It was the moment I had feared since hearing the news of the welfare's decision to send us to different homes.

I watched from the living room window as a kindly looking woman stepped out of the car. She was rather thin and wore a soft pink flowered dress. Besides her usual black briefcase, she carried a pink purse. Her blond hair hung in gentle curls around her face.

She knocked loudly and Richard Fletcher went to the door. "Hello," she greeted him warmly. "I'm Evelyn Johnson, from the St. Croix County Welfare Department. I have come to meet Ellie Brewster."

I wanted to run up to her and say she had the wrong farm, or that Ellie Brewster didn't live here...anything to keep this awful separation from happening. Instead, I sat on the couch in the living room, biting my nails, and feeling as weak as a wet noodle.

"Come in," Mr. Fletcher said. "I'll call Ellie. She's up in her room."

Mr. Fletcher walked to the bottom of the stairs and called my sister.

"Ellie, Mrs. Johnson has come for you now."

In a few moments, her bedroom door opened slowly. She walked down the steps carrying her cardboard box of personal belongings.

I followed her as she entered the kitchen. I saw Mrs. Johnson's beautiful smile. That smile seemed to bring some comfort into our sad situation. "Hello Ellie," she said in a soothing voice. "And is this your twin brother Eddie?"

Ellie didn't answer. She only nodded her head slightly. I could see that her tears were about to start again, and this time I figured I would cry, too.

"Mr. Fletcher, would you please sign these papers for Ellie?" Mrs. Johnson asked. "Right at the bottom will be fine, please. Thank you."

I had so many questions. Would I ever see Ellie again? Would the people she lived with make her feel like a family member or an outsider? Would they want her to live with them just to do their extra work?

As Ellie's tears trickled down her cheeks, Mrs. Johnson reached into her pink purse. "Here you are, Ellie, these are for you. I thought you might need them today."

Mrs. Johnson handed Ellie three lace trimmed handkerchiefs monogrammed with the pink letter "E".

"You see, Ellie, I was a foster girl once, too," Mrs. Johnson said. "I know how it feels to move from place to place. I cried a lot of tears after my mother and father died. But eventually, I grew up and found my place in life. You will too, honey. You will, too."

She sat for a moment and let Ellie cry into her handkerchief, gently patting her arm.

"Mrs. Johnson," I said. "Will I be able to find out where Ellie is living?"

"I will personally see that you will find out where she lives and who she lives with," she said to me with her kind smile.

I hoped that I could trust her. But I didn't even know where I was moving. I knew that only God would know where each of us went. The words that Mother Okerby said to us came back to my mind once again: *"Remember, God is with you wherever you go, and He hears your prayer."*

"Come then, my child. Give your brother a good big hug, and let's be off to new adventures. It isn't the last you'll see of each other, I promise," Mrs. Johnson said.

We hugged each other and cried because we had seen too many broken promises to believe for certain that we would ever meet again.

Chapter Eleven

"Well, let's get a good breakfast. What do you say, Eddie?" Mr. Fletcher said to me as we walked up to the house after our morning chores were finished.

"Yeah, I guess so," I answered without much enthusiasm.

"I know you're missing your sister. I'm going to be mighty lonely when you're both gone, you know."

"I can't see why the welfare wouldn't just let us live with you until your wife gets well," I said. "We get along okay here."

"They have their rules, and they aren't about to bend them for anyone."

As Richard Fletcher was busy frying bacon and eggs, the telephone rang. He answered it and was brought to the abrupt realization that today he would lose me, too.

"You're coming this morning? Well, okay...if that is your decision. Good bye." He hung up the phone and walked slowly back to the stove to serve our breakfast.

"It looks like they're going to come soon, Eddie...before lunch, in fact. Don't really know why they're in such a rush. Guess they want you settled in your new home before school starts."

All of a sudden this great bacon and eggs breakfast didn't seem fantastic. I felt that old queasy pitching begin in my stomach. Why did this have to happen again?

I like Richard Fletcher. I love working in his clean barn with his contented cows. Even though his wife isn't here, we could help each other and do a great job with his herd. I could be the kind of boy he needs, like the son he never had. He would be happy and so would I. "How come I can't stay?" I said aloud.

But then I realized: No, it's just like Mr. Fletcher says. The rules…always the rules. They would never allow a young kid like me to grow up in this home without a foster mother.

* * *

About eleven o' clock a black Chevrolet drove up in Richard Fletcher's driveway. A familiar looking woman wearing a brown suit stepped out of the car. The sun glinted off her reddish hair, which was braided tightly into a crown on top of her head.

"Oh, no," I said to myself as I peeked out the window in the living room. "I would recognize that hair and those dark rimmed glasses anywhere. It's her… Miss Westfield. How did I rate getting her to move me a second time?

Soon there was a rapid pounding at the back door. Richard Fletcher answered with his usual polite manner. "Come in," he said as she walked boldly past him and into the kitchen. She set her black briefcase on the table.

"I see you fixed your back step," Miss Westfield said curtly. "I nearly broke my ankle a couple of weeks ago."

"Eddie repaired it right away. He's a willing worker. He can do most anything you ask him to do. Just show him once and he does it well," Mr. Fletcher said.

"I'll need you to sign this paper for Eddie's removal from your home," Miss Westfield said. "Right there on that line, please."

"Then we'll need to be going. Must keep on schedule, you know. Do you have your box ready to go, Eddie?"

"Yes," I said.

"Then we're on our way. Sorry this placement didn't work out, Mr. Fletcher."

When we walked outside, Miss Westfield shook hands with Mr. Fletcher and then walked toward her car. I put down my box and shook his hand, too.

"Thanks for teaching me so much about your herd, sir. I really did enjoy working with them. I'm glad I got to see my calf, Half Pint, too. That was the best surprise ever. And Mr. Fletcher, maybe you should get yourself a dog…he could be a good companion to you, especially now when we're gone."

Richard Fletcher's eyes filled with sadness as he patted my shoulder. I picked up my box and walked to Miss Westfield's car. Looking back out the rear window, I saw this lonely farmer raise his hand to wave as he watched the car drive away.

Chapter Twelve

As Miss Westfield left the country road and turned onto the main highway, I decided it was time for me to ask the big question.

"Miss Westfield, where is my next home?"

Miss Westfield stopped the rhythmic tapping of her red fingernails on the steering wheel. Instead, she gripped the wheel firmly and scowled at me through the rear-view mirror.

"Oh, I remember you. You're the one with all the questions, aren't you? If you would exercise some patience, you would find out soon enough. I can tell you one thing for sure: you won't be the only child in this home."

Soon her fingernails began tapping on the wheel once again. I knew that this was all the information I would get.

After what seemed like many miles, we came to a bridge and a sign that read: Apple River. Miss Westfield drove over the bridge and soon I saw another sign that read: Somerset, Wisconsin. We drove out of the town and onto another country road.

After several miles, the car slowed down and turned onto a narrow gravel driveway. It was lined with tall, thick, pine trees limiting my vision to nothing but the dirt road ahead.

Finally, the long driveway opened up to a vegetable garden on my right. A large white house stood at the end of the driveway.

Surrounding three sides of the house grew a colorful stand of tall maple trees. A short distance from the house, across the driveway, stood an old red barn, a garage, a granary, and a machine shed.

I saw children running and playing with a black and white sheep dog. He left them and came running over to greet us as our car approached.

"Oh, no, they didn't tell me they had a dog," Miss Westfield said in a frustrated voice. "I don't trust dogs."

"He doesn't look mean," I said. "He's barking 'cause that's what dogs do."

I got out and the dog came right up and wagged his tail. I could tell we would be friends right away. I patted his head. Miss Westfield sat in the car and rolled down her window a bit.

She called out to the oldest looking boy. "Will you please get your mother? I don't trust your dog the way he jumps."

The boy giggled and said, "He won't hurt you."

Then he ran up to the house to get his mother.

Soon a thin, blond-haired woman came out the door. Two little girls followed her. The girls were obviously twins. Although they weren't dressed the same, their faces had identical smiles, and both had blond curls and deep blue eyes. This would make it difficult to tell one from another.

I noticed how careful the dog was around the little girls. He seemed so protective. I didn't think Miss Westfield had a reason to be afraid. However, she refused to leave her car.

She rolled down her window a bit more as the children's mother approached the car. "I'm Bernice Westfield, from the St. Croix County Welfare Dept. I brought you Eddie Brewster. But I'm not taking any chances with your big dog jumping around," she said. "I don't trust dogs so I'm staying here in my car where I feel safe."

"Hi. I'm Janet Wagner and this is our dog Chip. He is a good companion for our children. You would never have to be afraid of him."

"Well, what you say may be true, but I feel much safer in here. I will let the boy get his things, and then I'll be off. I like to keep to my schedule, anyway. Would you please sign these papers…right there on the bottom." She squeezed her clipboard with attached papers through the car window.

"Just a formality, you know. Keep's the records in order."

"Do you need help with anything, Eddie?" Mrs. Wagner asked.

"No, I just have one box," I answered. I reached into the back seat and got my things.

"Why don't you come in the house and I'll show you where you can unpack," Mrs. Wagner said to me. Then she handed the clipboard back to Miss Westfield through the car window.

"Thank you and good bye then, Mrs. Wagner," Miss Westfield said without giving me another look. She turned her car around and headed back out the long driveway. I hoped that would be the last I saw of Miss Westfield for a very long time.

Chapter Thirteen

I followed my foster mother into the house. The children were filled with curiosity and tramped along behind us into the large kitchen. The moment I entered, I saw a huge built-in cabinet that covered the far wall of this room. To the left of this cupboard, I noticed the entry to the living room. To the right side, I saw a stairway leading upstairs.

"Eddie, I want you to meet our children. These are the twins, Elizabeth and Laura. They are two years old." The twins hung onto their mother's skirt and carefully peeked out at me.

"This is James who is three. Next to him is Charles. He is four years old. Standing over by the stove is Nathan who is five, and Benjamin who is six."

I nodded and grinned at the children as their mother introduced each of them to me.

I continued to check out the room. I saw a sink and hand pump to my right, next to the refrigerator. To my left, beneath a row of kitchen windows, stretched a long, dark wooden table, surrounded by chairs, high chairs and stools.

The little children whispered and giggled as they looked at me, so I continued to smile at them. Benjamin wore a big, toothless, grin. I figured they didn't understand how I was supposed to fit in. Actually, I felt the same way. Why would a family of this size want another mouth to feed?

"I didn't quite know how to explain to the little ones about your coming," Janet Wagner said. "I don't think they understand that you'll be living with us. It may take time for them to get used to having you as part of the family."

"That's okay," I answered. I really didn't expect to be treated as a family member.

"John and Daniel, our seven and eight-year-old boys, are in the barn cleaning a calf pen right now," Mrs. Wagner continued. "You will meet them later. Mr. Wagner works as a construction worker during the day, so we don't see him until supper time."

That last bit of information gave me the big clue. I'm sure what they wanted was someone to help with the farm work. The boys were too young to do all the chores alone. If the father was gone all day, that would leave plenty of work for me.

"Come upstairs, Eddie. I will show you where to put your box."

I followed Mrs. Wagner up the narrow staircase to the second floor of the old farmhouse. The stairs creaked and the old flowered wallpaper was beginning to peel.

There were four bedrooms, each one leading off the hallway. These rooms were where the Wagner children slept.

"You can sleep on this cot next to the commode in this hall, Eddie. That way you'll hear the children call from their bedrooms at night when they need help to go potty. That will be one of your responsibilities, along with emptying the commode pot each morning."

I could feel I was quickly losing my privacy, and any personal space I used to have. I shoved my box under the cot and thought about my own room and the life I almost lived in the home of Richard Fletcher.

"You can put your pillowcase, sheet, and blanket on your bed now," Mrs. Wagner said, as she handed me the bedding. "Then it will be ready for you tonight after you help the little ones get ready for bed. When you're finished with your bed, come downstairs and I'll show you around the rest of the farm."

I peeked into the other bedrooms. They were small and the beds were messy. Clothes, books, and toys were left scattered about the rooms. I wondered if picking up the clutter in the little kid's bedrooms would become my responsibility, as well as becoming their nursemaid.

Chapter Fourteen

"We're out here, Eddie," Mrs. Wagner called to me from the back porch. "Let's walk down to the barn and you can meet John and Daniel."

The Wagner's red barn was quite the opposite of the one I left at Richard Fletcher's farm. This barn was old, dark, and smelly. It looked like no one had cleaned it for a long time.

"Hi boys," Mrs. Wagner said to her oldest children. "I want you to meet Eddie Brewster."

She turned to me and said: "This is John holding the shovel, and Daniel there with the pitch fork."

The boys looked at me and grinned.

"Hi guys," I said.

"The boys are trying to clean up this pen because Mr. Wagner bought a couple of new calves at a sale last weekend," Mrs. Wagner said. "You can help them until Mr. Wagner comes home. We'll have supper and after that he'll want you to milk cows with him."

I could see that my life would be planned out with one duty after another in this home. From morning until night, inside and out, I would be required to be a chore boy for both my new foster mother and father.

"How many cows do you milk?" I asked.

"I believe there are ten, now," Mrs. Wagner said. "We don't

have milking machines, so the morning milking has been taking my husband too long. He needs to get to his contracting work in town. It will be good to have you help with the milking from now on. You do know how to milk cows, don't you?"

"I haven't done it alone," I said.

"Well, you'll get used to it. The big boys can help you some. They're good workers, aren't you, kids?"

John and Daniel looked at each other, shrugged, their shoulders and smiled. Something about the uncertain look on their faces didn't assure me they'd be dependable.

Mrs. Wagner left the barn and there I stood. It seemed I needed to at least put on some different clothes to work in this muck, so I followed her out the door.

"I'll need my old clothes to work with the boys," I said.

"Oh yes," she said. "And there's a pair of my husband's old barn boots you can use sitting on the porch. Did the boys tell you where they're dumping the manure?"

"No, they didn't."

"There is a large manure pile behind the barn. Mr. Wagner has leaned a long plank against the pile. You have to carefully push the wheelbarrow up the plank and dump it off at the top. Be careful so it doesn't tip off to the side. That makes my husband angry.

"The boys will show you where the manure pile is, but they don't have strength enough to push the wheelbarrow up the plank by themselves. The pile has gotten too high. They'll be very glad to have your help with all this work. I guess we've been expecting too much from them."

I changed into my old clothes and put on the barn boots. As I entered the barn to survey the situation, I saw the boys left their work and were playing tag up in the haymow. When they saw me, they stopped their game and looked at me with sheepish grins.

"Hey guys," I said. "Come on down and show me where to dump this wheelbarrow."

They looked at each other and slowly climbed down the haymow ladder.

"We were just havin' some fun," Daniel said. "Before Dad gets home."

"He always has work for us to do." John said. "He thinks playing is for the little kids. We're old enough to work now."

"Well, your Mother said you would show me where to dump this wheelbarrow. Don't you think we'd better get going?" I tried to seem positive about the whole stinky mess.

"The manure pile is out behind the barn. Follow us," Daniel said. "The pile is getting tall, and we can't do it alone anymore."

"It's not an easy job," John warned me. "You have to be careful to keep your balance walking up the plank. If the wheelbarrow spills before it gets to the top, it just spreads out on the side. When that happened to us it made my dad mad. He wants us to push it right to the top and then dump it over out behind the pile. When we can't do it right, he yells a lot."

Who was this man? My newest foster father that I hadn't even met…seems I was in for another amazing adventure. He must have some high expectations of his children doing the farm work. But now he had me. The only problem was I was only twelve years old…not too tall…and only four years older than his eldest son.

Chapter Fifteen

I was thankful the wheelbarrow was not completely full for my first try at walking the plank. The manure pile was lumpy and the plank wobbly.

"John, step back from this pile in case this wheelbarrow dumps too soon," I said, as I moved slowly on my way up.

Within moments of my warning, a clump of manure dropped off the front edge of the wheelbarrow. It lodged onto the front wheel, setting off my motion. I lost my balance. Only half way up the plank, the first stinky load was lost...too soon.

"Yuk," cried John, who had not heeded my warning in time.

Clods of manure hit the young boy as he backed quickly away.

"You're not supposed to dump it there," he whined. "That's not the right way. Wait 'til my dad hears about this. He's gonna be mad. You got to do it like we said. We told you how."

"Quiet, John," Daniel said. "It's the first time he ever tried it. And never mind about Dad hearing about this. Eddie's just learning how to do it."

There was nothing to do but get another load and try again.

"Come on back to the barn, guys, let's see if we can finish that calf pen before your dad gets home," I said.

* * *

Mrs. Wagner called the family together for supper. I pumped the water into the wash basin in the sink. Next to the sink was a soap dish with a large golden-brown bar of soap. It didn't make a lot of suds on my hands, but it cleaned away the dirt of the stinky job we had accomplished. After I dried my hands, I hurried over to join the others.

The table bore large serving dishes of roast pork, potatoes, and gravy. A casserole held pieces of butternut squash with melted butter. Janet Wagner was a busy mother, especially at mealtime. She carefully dished portions for each of her small children. Then she began passing the serving dishes around to each of the older children.

The two-year-old twins sat in high-chairs next to their mother. Although these little girls looked exactly alike, their personalities were different.

Elizabeth, gentle and quiet, waited patiently for her food, and chewed on a piece of bread crust. Laura, on the other hand, rearranged life for everyone. She whacked her high-chair tray with her spoon. Either she expected food right now, or she enjoyed the rhythm her constant banging produced.

"I'll get the milk," Daniel said as he poured rich creamy milk fresh from this morning's milking into various sized plastic glasses. The Wagner family drank a lot of milk, all of it right from the cows they milked on their own farm.

We all ate the home cooked food with ravenous appetites, passing plates back and forth for second and third helpings.

"There are fresh cookies for dessert for those kids with clean plates," Mrs. Wagner said. "That means eat all your squash too, Benjamin."

"I know," Benjamin giggled. "Can I have two cookies?"

"Yes, everyone can have two."

As we were finishing our meal, I heard a car drive up into the driveway. A dark haired man of medium build walked into the kitchen. He was dressed in dusty, well-worn blue jeans and a plaid shirt.

"Eddie, meet my husband," Janet Wagner said.

"Hi," I said.

Mr. Wagner washed his hands at the pump and sat down at the table without a response to me or a greeting to anyone else.

"I've kept a plate warm for you, Donald," Mrs. Wagner said. "How was your day?" She handed him his plate, hot from the oven.

"Long." A silence came over the meal after his one-word answer. When he cleaned his plate, Mr. Wagner pushed his chair back from the table.

"Finish up," he said with a weary look. "We've got milking to do."

Milking on the Wagner farm was done by hand with no milking machines to save time. The barn was not a well kept barn and the barn cleaning efforts and repairs at the Wagner farm were done only to get by.

I saw that Daniel had an interest in the farm and worked willingly. I knew I could trust him to help me if I ever had to do the milking alone.

John, on the other hand, didn't care much about the outside chores. He could be counted on sometimes, but he would rather be playing with his younger brothers and sisters.

In the summer, Donald Wagner kept his cows pastured in the rich pastureland across the road at the end of their long driveway. This meant moving them back and forth before and after milking.

Chip, the Wagner's sheep dog helped us keep them in line as they plodded along their trip to the barn to be milked and then back again to freedom in the pasture.

* * *

"Eddie, I've hitched up the team this morning. I want you and the boys to bring back as many loads of corn bundles as you can when I'm at work," Mr. Wagner said with his usual sour look. "Be sure you drive the horses slowly when you're coming up the driveway so the bundles won't fly off. And have the cows up in the barn ready to be milked when I get home.

"School starts next week, so you won't be around during the day. We've got to get some more bundles hauled out of that field and stored in the barn. I'm expecting you to do it."

With that he put on his cap, grabbed his lunch bucket, and without even a goodbye, left us all sitting at the breakfast table.

"Eddie, before you haul bundles, you and I are making a trip to town. You need to have some new school shoes. We will leave as soon as the stores open. My friend is coming to stay with the children while we shop. We won't mention this to Mr. Wagner. It's something I promised your social worker I would do when she called last week.

"You'll have time to walk the cows back out to the pasture right now, before we leave. Daniel and John can help with the cows, too."

"Here Chip…" I called as I walked out the back door. I only had to call once and Chip came bounding around the barn. He knew his job as we prepared to walk the cattle back to pasture. Always running along side, weaving in-between those cows that would wander, he kept them together, and watched them so they didn't get too far ahead.

Chip knew the danger of the road. Even with the sign posted: *"Cattle Crossing,"* some cars didn't slow down.

"John, you go ahead and open the pasture gate," I said, as we approached the road.

70

As the gate swung open I looked both ways and saw a clear roadway.

"Let's go," I said to Daniel. We began bringing the cattle across. Chip, with his firm yet gentle herding motion, kept the cows moving together in the right direction.

When we had the critters nearly across, it seemed a black-pick up approached out of nowhere. I expected to see this vehicle begin to slow down. Instead, it appeared to gain speed swerving from one lane to the other.

"Move girl," I shouted to Josie, our lead cow. "Move! C'mon, Move!

"Boys, Get off the road," I yelled.

Chip began to bark. He ran around behind the last cow and nipped at her hooves and barked and barked. The cows picked up their trot to a run as the last cow cleared the road just in time.

The racing black pick-up with its crazy driver had nearly killed the cows and us boys too. He surely must have seen us. I could taste the anger mounting in my throat as I looked to the side of the road. What a rotten, careless, irresponsible driver.

I dropped down beside the limp body of my black and white friend. He had done all he could do to save us. If he hadn't gotten behind the last cow to bark and prod her along, he would be alive today.

Chapter Sixteen

"Run up to the house and tell your mother," I said, my voice husky and choked with tears. "I'll stay here with Chip."

As the boys ran up the driveway to bring the sad news to their mother, I poured out my broken heart to my Heavenly Father.

"Dear God, why did Chip have to die? Couldn't you let him live like you did for my little Half-Pint?"

As I thought and prayed about this whole situation, Mrs. Wagner walked down the driveway toward me with the wheelbarrow.

"I left the big boys with the other kids," she said. "I thought maybe you and I could put Chip in the wheelbarrow and bring him back to the house. The kids will want to see him again. We can find a good spot to bury him out behind the barn. John and Daniel will help us do that." She set the wheelbarrow down and wiped her eyes.

"I feel terrible. He was the best dog we ever had. I know my husband thinks a dog is just a dog. But when you're out here alone on this farm everyday, you need to have a dog you can trust."

I saw the tears spill out of Mrs. Wagner's eyes as she knelt down and buried her face into Chip's black and white coat. "I loved you, dear dog," she said as she patted him gently. "And I'll miss you..."

Suddenly she sat up. She placed her hand over the dog's chest.

"This dog isn't dead. He's breathing. Come here, Eddie...see if you can feel his heartbeat."

I placed my hand in Chip's soft fur and felt a weak but steady thump.

"Let's get him into the wheelbarrow. Easy now, we have to go slow. We'll get the boys to bring some straw and make him a fresh bed in the barn. Maybe with some rest and time...we can only wait and see what happens."

* * *

"Hi Gertie," Mrs. Wagner said as a tall, slender, brown-haired woman entered the kitchen. "Come on in. I want you to meet Eddie Brewster, the newest member of our family."

"Hi Eddie," Gertie Lou said with a bright smile.

"Eddie, this is my friend and neighbor Gertrude Louise Holt. Everyone calls her Gertie Lou."

"Nice to meet you," I said.

"We've had quite a morning around here, Gertie," Mrs. Wagner continued. "I almost thought of canceling our trip to town."

"What happened?" Gertie asked.

"We almost lost Chip. Some reckless driver didn't slow down when the kids were moving the cattle across the road. Seems he didn't see the cattle crossing signs on the road. He was swerving from lane to lane and going too fast.

"Anyway, he nearly hit the kids and the cows. Chip was trying to protect everyone and got hit," Janet said. "That's our Chip, always working and watchful."

"Aren't you going to call Doc Rolf?"

"I'm going to stop and talk to him when Eddie and I go to town. Donald worries about spending money for the vet when we don't need to. He'd be angry if I called him out here and Chip died anyway.

"We made a bed for him inside the barn. Daniel and John are with him now. They will stay with him until we get back. We'll continue to watch him and hope that the rest and quiet will help him come around.

"Thanks for staying with the kids and letting me use your car. I'm going to report that driver to the police, too. I won't be gone long.

"Let's go Eddie," Janet Wagner said. "The sooner we get to town, the sooner we can see the vet."

"Have you been friends with Gertie Lou for a long time?" I asked when we got into the car and started on our way to town.

"Gertie Lou and her husband owned the farm next to ours for about ten years. He died a year ago from cancer. She decided to continue living on the farm and she rents out the farm land. She sold the milk cows but keeps a herd of beef steers. The Holt's were never able to have children of their own, so they always enjoyed spending time with us and our family. She's like an aunt to my children and a dear friend to me."

For a while we rode in silence and my thoughts returned to Chip. It would be a sad day for the Wagner family if they lost their faithful friend. I had just met this loyal pooch, but he already captured my heart.

Chapter Seventeen

"Mrs. Wagner, will we be going to the Vet's office first thing?" I asked my foster mother.

"We will, Eddie," she said. "He's a good doctor and if there's anything he can do, he'll let me know."

We drove down Main Street and parked in front of a brick building. A sign on the lawn read:

SOMMERSET VETERNARY CLINIC
Dr. Frank Rolf, DVM

We hurried out of the car into the building. The smell in this clinic seemed to be a mixture of pine scent and antiseptic. I figured the pine scent must be floor cleaner. A sign in the hallway read: CAUTION—WET FLOOR.

Holly Davis, a friendly receptionist, greeted us as we approached the desk.

"Hello. May I help you?" she asked.

"I'm Janet Wagner and this is Eddie Brewster. We just need a few minutes of Dr. Rolf's time. Our dog was hit by a car this morning and I want to ask him some questions. Is he in the office?"

"Oh, I'm sorry about your dog. Dr. Rolf is here right now, but he's going out on a farm call in a few minutes. I'll ask him if he can see you before he leaves. "

"Thank you."

We sat down in the quiet waiting room. I picked up a magazine with a beautiful horse on the cover. I'd like to own a horse like that, I thought to myself. One I could train and ride. The pictures in this magazine hardly seemed real. I'd never seen such a fancy saddle and bridle.

"Mrs. Wagner and Eddie, you can come back now," the receiptionist said. I laid the magazine down and followed Mrs. Wagner into Dr. Rolf's office.

In this room were scenes of wildlife both in paintings and taxidermy. A ten point buck, white-tail deer head hung on the wall over Dr. Rolf's desk. Several pheasant and ducks were set on top of file cabinets. I guessed this doctor would be as much at home in the woods as he was caring for sick animals.

"Good morning, folks. Holly tells me your dog was hit by a car?" Dr. Rolf said as he entered his office dressed in cowboy boots, jeans, and a blue and white plaid shirt.

"Yes, he was. Chip is like part of our family. I trust him as a protector in the yard to watch out for our little ones. Eddie and the older boys depend on his help with the cattle. But Donald is so worried about our vet bill... I feel I can't ask you to come out to the house and see Chip."

"Now just a minute," Doc Rolf said. He set his glasses down on his desk, and smoothed out his slightly graying beard. "Donald pays regularly on your vet bill. I know your family is trying to do the right thing. Tell you what. I'm just about to leave on a farm call out your way. I'll swing by your place and take a look at the dog. We'll see what we can do for him. Right now, the best you can do is keep him quiet and I'll see you out there in a couple of hours."

I noticed a slight smile and a look of relief as Mrs. Wagner shook Doc Rolf's hand. Then he reached out for my hand, too.

"Looks like you'll be a great help out at the Wagner farm," he said, as he shook my hand warmly.

I smiled and nodded.

We hurried to Gertie Lou's car and drove to Swanson's Family Shoe Store. This building was a block off Main Street.

The sign in the window read: FOR THE BEST FIT, SHOP SWANSON'S FAMILY SHOE STORE... FAMOUS FOR OUR FLUOROSCOPE MACHINE!

"I want you to get a good fit in your new shoes," Janet Wagner said. "The welfare funds will pay for this pair, so they should be the best."

"Hello," said a man's voice. "I'm James Swanson." A tall salesman with a thick gray moustache walked from behind a shelf of shoe boxes. He was dressed in a dark gray suit and striped black and white tie.

"Shoes for you, Madam? Or for the boy?" He spoke in a most polite manor.

"We're buying shoes for Eddie," Mrs. Wagner said.

"Sit down, son," he said. "Let's check your size. What type of shoes are you interested in?"

"I think they should be sturdy leather shoes...they will be school shoes," Mrs. Wagner said.

"I think I have a couple of styles you may be interested in. I'll get them and you can see which pair you like best. After you slip the shoes on, we'll have you step into our fluoroscope machine, and then you can see for yourselves how the shoes fit."

When Mr. Swanson went to find the shoes for me, I looked at the displays advertising black leather service shoes built specifically for postmen, policemen, firemen, and railroad men. The ad said they would be durable as well as comfortable.

Another rack displayed BUSTER BROWN shoes...*a sturdy shoe for little feet that run, jump, and play.* HIPPITY HOPS were advertised for little girls to wear... They come in two choices! Pick Your Favorite...tan leather and black patent leather. The sign said: "*Room for little feet to grow...cool, new, and smart. Bring in your little gal today.*"

I noticed Mrs. Wagner carefully pick up a fashion high heeled shoe, with an admiring look on her face. She gently ran her hand across the delicate bow and its shiny patent leather surface. She looked as if she wished to try on this elegant pair.

At that moment Mr. Swanson's voice brought her back to reality.

"I think you'll like what I have here."

The shoe with the bow slipped from her hand onto the floor. She quickly picked it up and came over to see the shoes he selected for me.

Mr. Swanson slipped the shoes on easily with his silver shoe horn which he kept in his suit jacket pocket. He laced the shoes up comfortably.

"Step up into our machine, young man," he said. "Let's see how those look."

I looked down through the view port and saw the bones in my feet through a mysterious light-green glow. I wiggled my toes, and sure enough, the toes in the machine wiggled, too. So it really must be my foot, I thought.

Mrs. Wagner came over to view my feet.

"Seems there is quite enough room around his toes, wouldn't you say?" she said to Mr. Swanson.

"I do believe so. I also have this style in brown. There is another type with a scuff-proof Sharkskin tip, but it is a dressier shoe. Would you be interested in seeing that style, also?"

"No, I don't think that sounds appropriate for a school shoe do you Eddie?"

"I like the black one I have on," I said.

"Then that's the pair we will take."

"Okay, I'll get this pair boxed up for you," Mr. Swanson said.

"Thanks," Janet Wagner said. "And we'll get on our way."

As we approached Gertie Lou's car to hurry home, I stopped short.

"Mrs. Wagner, we're not going anywhere right now…take a look at this back tire."

Chapter Eighteen

"Oh, honestly! That's not what we need now. I want to get right home to be there when Doc Rolf comes by," Janet Wagner said. "See if there's a jack in the trunk. Maybe we could take the flat tire off and put on the spare, then run the flat up to Ron's Mobile on the corner and have it fixed."

I looked in the trunk, but the jack was gone.

"There's no jack here, "I said.

"Let's walk up to the station and see if we can borrow a jack. We've just got to get home."

"Can I help you folks?" a smiling station attendant greeted us.

"We were parked in front of the shoe store down the street and came out to a flat tire," Mrs. Wagner said. "Do you have a jack we could borrow?"

"We sure do, ma'am. I'm thinking' if this young man can get the tire off for you, you can bring it up here and we'll fix it. You'll be out of here within the hour."

"That would be great," Mrs. Wagner said.

"Oh, by the way, we're celebrating our station's twenty-fifth anniversary this week. We're giving out a souvenir to deserving customers. You would fit into that category, my boy."

I noticed the station attendant's name badge said "Phil." He looked at me with one of his generous smiles, and then he reached his large hand underneath the counter into a cardboard box. Out came a metal replica of Mobile's symbol of the "flying red horse."

"Thank you, Phil." I said.

"You're most welcome, I'm sure," he said with another large grin. "Stop back and see us again if we can help you in any way."

"We'd better hurry up then," Mrs. Wagner said. "And thanks for the use of the jack."

* * *

With the tire repaired, we had one stop left to make.

"I want to stop by the police station and tell them about that driver. In case someone else has spotted him," Mrs. Wagner said.

I waited in the car for my foster mother, and in a few minutes she was back in the car. "It seems someone else along our road also called in about that crazy driver. I'm just glad we reported it, too. I hope they catch him."

"Did they get a license number?" I asked.

"No. So far, he's been driving too fast for anyone to see it."

"Sure hope we haven't missed Doc Rolf," Janet Wagner said. "I'll feel better when I know he has looked at Chip."

"Do you think Chip is going to make it?" I asked.

"I know we have done all we can do for him," she said. "That's all anyone can do."

"I'm praying for Chip," I said. "My first foster mother told me that I could pray to God wherever I was, and God would hear my prayer. I believe it's true. Once when my twin sister was lost in a snowstorm, I prayed that I would find her before she froze to death and I found her. I believe God answered my prayer."

"When I was a little girl, my parents took me to church," Mrs. Wagner said. "Our family prayed too. Then my parents died in a car crash. I was lonely and sad. My aunt and uncle took me to live with them, and they didn't pray, and we never went to church. I figured God forgot about me. When I grew up, I married Donald Wagner. He isn't interested in church or any of that God-stuff. I don't pray or think about God anymore. I try to be the best person I can, and I take good care of my kids. They're my life now."

"Oh." I felt bad for Janet Wagner. She could think what she wanted, but I knew God answered my prayer. Maybe sometime she will pray again, too.

"Well, we're home, Eddie. Let's go see how Chip is doing…"

"Yeah, I sure hope he's still alive."

Mrs. Wagner shut the car off and we hurried toward the barn.

"Mom, come quick," John called from the barn door.

We hurried and found Chip's eyes open. He gave us a gentle whimper and a slight wag of his tail.

Mrs. Wagner dropped to her knees and softly stroked Chip's coat.

"Good boy, you're going to get better, aren't you?"

I heard a car drive into the driveway, and within moments Doc Rolf joined us in the barn.

"How's your dog doing, Mrs. Wagner?" he asked.

"His eyes are open, and he moved his tail. He even whimpered a bit."

"Those are all good signs," Doc Rolf said. "I'll examine him and see what injuries he has."

We all watched as he gently checked Chip's limbs and head for broken bones, and then he listened to his heart and lungs.

"Chip has suffered a large bruise on the left side of his head. There's a great amount of swelling in this area. His left pupil does not react to light. I'm concerned he may lose the sight in that eye. The fact that he is responding well to your encouragement, is a positive sign. Keep him resting…that will be the best medicine. He's taken a hard hit, but he has no broken bones.

"I'll be out this way again tomorrow. I'll stop by then. It's right on my way so please, not a word of concern over these visits."

He tipped his western hat to Mrs. Wagner, "Remember, keep him quiet. Good day then."

Chapter Nineteen

Mr. Wagner harnessed Queen and Bess, his two work horses, and left them in their stalls before going into town to his construction job. After milking, he thought I would hitch the horses to the wagon. Then through out the day, the boys would help me bring in loads of corn bundles from the field and stack them in the barn.

However, after Chip's accident, our trip to town, and the flat tire, our whole day seemed to melt away. When we actually got the team hitched to the wagon and on our way to the field, it was the middle of the afternoon.

I was glad the Wagner's owned such a gentle team of horses. They were reliable and hardworking, and I knew I could depend on them. They let me hitch them to the wagon with no bother, even though I was a new kid on the farm.

"Hey, Eddie, why did you move to our house?" John asked as we got started on our slow wagon ride to the field.

"When you're a foster kid like I am, you move a lot," I said. "Your place just happened to be the next one."

"Don't you have your own family?" Daniel asked.

"I was born into a large family. My mom got sick and died. My dad didn't have a job, so he couldn't take care of all of us. I became a foster kid. I had a twin sister that lived with me at the other foster families, but now I don't even know where she is."

"Well, you could be part of our family now, couldn't you?" Daniel asked.

"No. A foster kid always has to move on."

"See those purple thistles?" I said pointing to a large stand of thistles along the driveway.

"Yeah. What about 'em?" John asked.

"See this scar?"

Both boys saw the white horseshoe ridge on my left index finger, and looked at me wide-eyed.

"If you ever go cutting thistles, make sure you don't hold the thistle with your left hand and come down on it with a scythe in your right hand."

"You did that?" Daniel asked.

"Yup, I did."

"How many stitches did you have to get?" John asked.

"None. The old man I was living with said he wouldn't waste a trip to the doctor for a foster kid. Especially one that did something as stupid as cut his own hand. He put udder ointment on it with his dirty finger, and then he bandaged it up. His wife told me not to get it wet. Somehow it healed."

We neared the end of the driveway. John jumped off the wagon and crossed the road to open the gate.

"Okay, come on across," John called.

The warm afternoon sun beat down and I could hear the meadowlarks call in the pasture. It made me feel lazy, but I knew we had work to do. We'd better get at least one load of bundles back up to the barn before Donald Wagner gets home from work, I thought. He doesn't seem like the kind of man whose word I dare ignore.

"Well boys, let's load the wagon as fast as we can. We're getting a late start on the job your dad gave us to do."

"It's not our fault Chip got hit," John said.

"No, it's not anyone's fault but that maniac driver," I agreed.

We pulled at the bundles in the corn shocks one by one, and then lifted them up on the wagon. Each time I threw a bundle on the pile, I could feel another puff of dust bounce up and mix with the dribbles of sweat on my face.

John and Daniel worked hard, too. For being such young boys, they both wanted to do their best to keep up with me. As the pile of bundles inside the wagon increased, it meant tossing each one higher to get it to settle in.

"Hey guys," I said as I watched their efforts. Your bundles hit the wagon side, and then they slide back down to the ground. How about you pull the bundles out of the shock, and I'll throw them onto the wagon?"

"Okay," Daniel said.

John continued to fight with the bundle he was trying to toss into the wagon. He was determined he could do it by himself.

"You're just wasting time, and Dad will get home soon," Daniel yelled at his younger brother. "Come and help me pull these bundles out of this shock."

I drove the team over to the last few shocks. With the boys help, we were able to toss enough bundles in the wagon for our first load.

"Remember what my dad said about driving slow," John said, as he jumped down from the wagon to open the gate for us go through.

"Eddie knows what he has to do," Daniel yelled at his brother. "He always wants to sound like a know-it-all," Daniel said to me, as John stayed behind to fasten the gate.

"Giddiyap," I called to the horses, as John climbed up in the wagon seat.

Bess and Queen responded to my command and began their homeward plod, trudging heavily on the long gravel driveway.

Suddenly, out of the long grass in the driveway ditch, a loud whoosh and a flurry of feathers flew up just missing Queen's right eye. The unsuspecting whirring sound spooked the normally gentle horse and set her off into a fearful fit.

"A stupid grouse…" I said and I tried to hold back on the reins.

Queen reared up and whinnied, as she planted her front feet hard on the gravel drive. In panic, she bolted ahead and set the pace for Bess as well. Now there was no stopping either of them. I tried hard to hold back on the reins, but they intended on finding security in the barn.

"Hang on to the wagon, kids," I said. "I can't stop this team. If you fall out, you're going to get hurt bad."

From the corner of my eye, I could see some of the bundles were falling out of the wagon. I was more concerned that John and Daniel wouldn't fall off the wagon than any of our load. We could always go back later and pick up the bundles that fell.

When we reached the barn, the horses came to an abrupt stop. I turned around only to realize we were being followed. Donald Wagner jumped out of his car. The look on his face made me wish I could be any where else at that moment. I slid down from the wagon seat and stood holding the reins in my hand.

"What in the name of God's green earth are you doing, you stupid kid? Didn't I tell you not to run this team?" he yelled, as he grabbed the reins from me.

At that moment I noticed John and Daniel jump off the wagon seat and run into the house as fast as their bare feet would carry them.

"Did you see this driveway?" he growled. "Why do you think I told you to take it slow? Now look at this mess."

"But sir, a grouse flew up and spooked Queen…it almost hit her in the eye," I said. "I did not run the team on purpose."

"You dumb kid. You expect me to believe that? My team is gentle. They don't spook. And you're a liar, too. Making up stories about birds scaring my team, just 'cause you got caught running my horses. You turn around and I'll teach you to lie to me."

With that he whipped me good with the reins he held in his hand. I turned my back to him and hung onto the wagon box. I was another man's whipping boy...with another foster father that chose not to believe the truth.

Chapter Twenty

For days after my beating, Donald Wagner would not look at me. I did my chores and helped him milk morning and night. The boys helped, too. He said only a few words to them, but he never spoke directly to me.

After each milking, I spent a little time with Chip. He thrived on the attention that everyone gave him. But since he couldn't see out of his left eye, he was cautious about leaving the safety of the barn.

"That dog is near useless now that he's blind," Donald Wagner announced as he came home from work one evening. "He's going to be skittish. You mark my word. There's not much that can be done but put him down. It's what should have been done the first day he was hit."

"Donald, I can't believe you're saying that," Mrs. Wagner said with alarm. "We're all seeing improvement every day. Yesterday he barked when Gertie Lou's car drove in. You expect too much. He'll come around."

"I'll give 'em a week. If he doesn't improve and come out of the barn and act like a real watch dog, that's it. I'm not feeding a sickly, whimpering half-blind old hound that's not worth his keep."

"I wish you wouldn't talk like that in front of the children," Janet said. "Chip is their pet."

"They got ears. Let'em hear what life is like. A dog is a dog."

I noticed the children's faces take on an awful sober look. Supper was served and eaten in an extra measure of silence. Only the clicking of the spoons in the serving dishes and fresh milk being poured into glasses was an audible sound that rose above the gloomy mental picture that Donald Wagner draped over his family's supper table.

* * *

At night I was expected to help with the children. If one of the little one's needed to go potty during the night, the child called me for assistance. At bedtime, I got their pajamas on and sent them off to their beds. Mrs. Wagner rested a lot after supper. I figured it was because she had such a large family and cooked big meals and did a lot of dishes. She must have been tired. She was always pleasant to me and thanked me for what I did.

"Eddie, will you please get the little ones ready for bed early tonight?" Mrs. Wagner said when I came in from the barn. "I'm not feeling well, and they have been so wild today."

"Kids, your mother says it's bedtime," I told them after I washed up at the kitchen sink

"We don't want to go to bed yet," Benjamin said.

"I'll read you a story. The first one upstairs gets to choose the book," I said. With that, Benjamin ran as fast as he could and picked out "*The Complete Tales of Beatrix Potter*"...of course his favorite story was *The Tale of Benjamin Bunny*.

"I want to pick a story," Jimmy whined. "Benjamin always gets to pick first."

"It's early, maybe we'll have time for two stories if you get your pajamas on fast and quit fighting," I said. "All kids with pajamas on, come and sit on the floor in the boy's bedroom and I'll read. I'll show everyone the pictures if nobody fights or pushes."

"What's rabbit-tobacco made of?" asked John. "I can't remember."

"It's made of ground up lavender," Daniel said. He had heard the Beatrix Potter stories a great many times in his young life.

At that moment, I heard Janet Wagner call me downstairs.

"Eddie, something is terribly wrong. I'm having sharp pains in my abdomen. I'm thinking I may be pregnant again. Donald is taking me in to the hospital. You will need to stay with the children and get them to bed. Please don't say anything to them about the possibility of a new baby. I wouldn't want them to be told that unless it really was true.

"Donald will be back as soon as he can and let you know what is happening. If you need anything, call Gertie Lou. Her number is by the telephone. She will come and help if you have an emergency."

"Okay," I said.

I went back upstairs to the kids. As I walked into the boy's room, a pillow sailed toward my head. I reached out and caught it. The look on John's face declared his guilt.

"John, get over here and sit down if you want to listen to this story. Stop the pillow fight right now."

"Benjamin started it first."

"It doesn't matter who started it. I'm ending it. Now if you want me to read these stories, sit down or it will be too late for even one of them."

"We need a big kid's story," John said. "I'm tired of little kid's stuff."

"Would you like to hear a story about a giant-killer?" I asked. "I could read you one about a boy that saved a whole army. His only weapon was a slingshot and five smooth stones."

"Yeah, I want to hear that one," John said with excitement in his voice.

"Me, too," Daniel said. "Is that story in that big book in your box?"

"It sure is," I said

I paused as I heard muffled voices from downstairs that led me to believe someone was speaking on the telephone. I heard the words: "Bertha, we really need you to come and stay a while... Janet may need to be in the hospital. But I'll let you know," I heard Mr. Wagner say. Then he hung up. A short conversation took place as the Wagner's shut the backdoor. Then all was quiet.

Outside the car started, and soon the sound of the motor faded as the car drove down the driveway. I figured I was on my own now.

"Let's read *The Tale of Benjamin Bunny* first," Benjamin said.

"Yes, that's what we're going to do," I said. But in my mind, I wondered *"who's Bertha?"* What in the world is going to happen next in this unique foster family?

As we read this story written by Beatrix Potter, I realized that Mrs. Wagner must have read frequently to her children. They all seemed fascinated with the antics of Benjamin and his cousin Peter Rabbit, and they cheered when the rabbits escaped from Mr. McGregor's garden. The pictures in the Beatrix Potter book were as delightful as the stories were to these children. We passed the book back and forth, letting everyone see the pictures.

"Now read us the story about the giant-killer," John said impatiently.

"Okay, that's what I'll do," I said. "I have to go and get my book in the box under my bed. Is everyone ready to hear an exciting story?"

"Yes, we are," the children agreed.

"This is the story: God's people, the Israelites, and their enemies the Philistines were at war. There was a huge Philistine warrior whose name was Goliath. He was a wicked giant, taller and meaner than anyone. Because of his size, every soldier in the army of Israel was afraid of him. King Saul couldn't find even one volunteer to fight this giant.

Then a young shepherd boy named David came to visit his three brothers who were soldiers in the Israelite army. When David heard Goliath come out to jeer at the people of God, as he did every morning and every evening, the Spirit of God stirred the shepherd boy's heart and filled him with courage.

"Why should this wicked Philistine trouble us?" David asked bravely. "I will go out and fight him. God has allowed me to kill both a lion and a bear to protect my father's sheep. God will deliver Goliath into my hands, and I will kill him."

When Goliath saw the young boy David coming to fight him, he said: "Am I a dog that you have come to fight against me with that staff?"

But David replied: "You have come to me with a sword, and with a spear, and with a shield; but I come to you in the name of the Lord of hosts, the God of the armies of Israel, which you have mocked."

Then this young man went to the brook and picked up five smooth stones. He placed one in his sling and swung it around and around and around. Then zing it sailed right into the center of the giant's forehead, and he fell down dead. The Philistines turned and ran back to their own land because they knew God was helping the people of Israel."

"Wow, that's an amazing story!" John said. "Is it true?"

"Yes. It's a Bible story," I said. "We can pray and ask for God's help with our problems, like He helped David fight the giant.

"Okay, kids. It's time to get to bed. Tomorrow is another day. We'd better be ready for it."

Chapter Twenty-One

"Eddie, I need to go potty again," Charles said, as he walked by me to the commode.

"Okay."

Charles finished quickly and stopped by my bed.

"Eddie, will you be living with us forever?"

"Forever is a long time, Charles," I said. "I 'spose I'll move again because that's what foster kids do."

"What's a floster kid?"

"It's foster not floster. A kid that lives with another family when he can't live with his own family is called a foster kid. Kids in the foster care system often move from one family to another. But now it's time for you to get back into bed...goodnight, Charles."

I heard his little bare feet run back into the boy's room. Quiet loneliness settled over this house like a thick quilt.

All this talk about families got me thinking again about my own life.

I wonder if I have brothers and sisters living somewhere in the world? When Ellie and I learned the family secret from Mother and Father Okerby, we were told there were other children in the Brewster family. I wonder where they are? Do I have an older brother or two? Maybe I have older sisters? I wonder if they have blond hair like me, or brown hair like Ellie? Worst thing is I don't even know where they took Ellie.

I climbed out of my bed and peeked into the older boy's room. They were asleep. I checked on Elizabeth and Laura and the younger boys. They were asleep as well.

I quietly slipped downstairs and carefully opened the back door. The moon brightened the sky as I walked quietly toward the barn.

I jumped at the hoot of an owl in a nearby tree. It sounded so close it could have been on my shoulder. Then I heard it...a low, fierce, growl. It was coming from the direction of the barn. I hoped it was what I had been waiting for.

"Please God, let that be Chip. I don't care if he snaps at me," I said quietly. "Please let him get his watch-dog spunk back and prove his worth to Mr. Wagner."

I crept closer, trying not to let on who I was. The deep throated snarl persisted as I noticed a dark form appear in the shadows. With a threatening leap, the protector broke loose and ran toward me.

"Chip," I cried. "It's me."

Chip stopped. His menacing look dissolved in the dust of the driveway, and his shaggy tail began to wag. He came running toward me for my usual hug and pat on the head.

"Good boy! Good watch dog. That's just what you have to do. Just like before."

I could see a car coming on the highway. What if it was Mr. Wagner? I better get in the house if it was. He might not like the idea of me being out here with Chip.

"You're a good boy, Chip," I said. "You bark every time a car comes in this driveway. It will save your life."

I gave Chip another hug and ran into the house. I hurried up the steps and got back into my bed listening for any indication that it was Mr. Wagner's car that I had seen.

Suddenly the quiet night erupted into a hullabaloo of barking, growling, and snarling. I could hear a man's voice curse loudly followed by a dog's squealing yelp. The back door slammed and Mr. Wagner stood at the bottom of the steps and called my name:

"Eddie, come down here," he said with a gruff snarl.

I came downstairs confused at what I surmised had happened.

"That fool dog goes from a spineless wimp to a vicious maniac. He doesn't even know his owner. I kicked him in the head. Stupid thing. I'll put him down in the morning."

"But sir, maybe he couldn't see you because of his blind eye," I said. "Besides, didn't you want him to be a watchdog again?"

I figured I was getting myself in deep, but it was my only chance to defend my friend Chip. Right now I felt that old feeling of wanting to run away, and this time I'd take Chip with me.

"I don't have time to talk about a dimwitted, no-good, dog now. Mrs. Wagner's going to be in the hospital for a while. My sister Bertha is coming here to stay with the family. The kids can't get along with her, and I don't either. She doesn't like being here, that's for sure…but it's all we can do. She'll be here in two days.

"Gertie Lou will come over tomorrow and be with the little ones. She'll get you started on washing the clothes. But we gotta get this place cleaned up because my sister Bertha is a hateful nag. You'll see what I mean. It won't be fun having her telling us what to do all the time. Now you'd better get back to bed. You got a lot of work to do when you get up."

Chapter Twenty-Two

I got up early to help Mr. Wagner do the milking and the calf chores. I noticed Chip kept his distance from him. After Mr. Wagner left for work, I finished up in the barn and went inside the house to get the kids going on breakfast.

Within the hour, a loud barking let us know that someone drove into the yard. It was Gertie Lou, and Chip realized quickly that she was a friend, so his warning was brief.

Gertie Lou had a way of making everyone's day brighter.

"Hi, Elizabeth, and Laura...come and see Gertie Lou."

The twins giggled and climbed up on their friend's lap.

"I'll bet you girls are missing your mommy, aren't you?" she said, as she hugged both of them while she talked to the rest of us.

"If any of you need anything while your Mom is gone, you know you can call me.

"I'll help you figure out what we can do to get this house in order before your Aunt Bertha comes."

She assigned jobs to each of us. Even Elizabeth and Laura did their part. Gertie Lou gave each of the twins a dust rag and let them dust the books and the lower book shelves in the living room.

"Daniel, you take Nathan and James for your team. John, you take Benjamin and Charles for your team. Both teams go upstairs and start cleaning your bedrooms. Put all your toys in the toy boxes, and put all the books on the book shelves. Then get the carpet sweeper and broom. Look for cobwebs, and then make your beds with fresh sheets.

"Eddie and I will supervise and do the big cleaning downstairs here. We have to scrub the kitchen floor, dust the light fixtures, look for cob webs, dust the furniture, and carry out garbage and all the scrap from the waste baskets."

"You know that Aunt Bertha hates us," John said. "Nobody could be that mean and not hate us."

"Oh, that's not true," Gertie Lou said, as she made sandwiches for all of us at lunchtime. "She never had the privilege of having children so she doesn't know how delightful you all are. Maybe this time, if she stays longer, she'll get to know each of you."

"I hope she doesn't stay long," Daniel said. "My dad gets surly after she's told him off a few times. Then he takes it out on us. And besides, he says they never got along when they were kids either."

"Aunt Bertha says we got too many kids," John said. "And that makes my mom cry."

The question that continued to pry at my mind was, why would anyone as mean as they say Aunt Bertha is, be coming to here to help them? It appeared that I would soon find out the answer to my question.

"We're going to tackle washing the clothes after lunch, Eddie," Gertie Lou said. "Daniel and John, you bring down all the dirty clothes from upstairs and take them to the basement."

Gertie Lou helped me sort the mounds of dirty clothes into piles by their colors. All the white clothes were put in one pile.

"We'll wash these white clothes first, Eddie," she said, as we filled the round Maytag wringer washer with the hottest water we could stand.

"You can add a scoop of the Oxydol laundry detergent from

the box on that shelf. Then add bleach to whiten and freshen the load," she said.

I watched the white clothes swish about as the agitator in the machine whipped them around. The suds formed a mound high above the top of the machine. After ten minutes of whirling in the hot soapy water, the clothes were ready to be rinsed. Gertie Lou showed me how to send the clothes through the wringer and into the tub of rinse water.

"Always watch where your fingers are, Eddie, so you don't get them in the wringer. That really hurts. It's happened to me, so I know. If the clothes bunch up or your fingers get caught, slam this release bar really hard. Then the rollers of the wringer will release their pressure," Gertie Lou said.

Yikes! I thought, that sounds awful. I continued to rinse the clothes up and down, and then I sent each item through the wringer into the second rinse tub.

"Now we have to rinse them once more in the last rinse water," she said. In this last rinse tub I sloshed the clothes a bit more, separating them carefully. I ran each piece of clothing through the wringer, into the clothes basket, and then carried them out to the clothes line to dry.

I did the load of light colored clothes, the darker load, followed by the dirtiest load of work clothes, these all followed the white clothes, each with their double rinse process. Then the dirty water in the machine was ready to be sent down the floor drain. I rinsed out the washing machine too so it would be fresh for the next use.

John, Daniel, and Gertie Lou helped me hang the wash on the clothesline in the back yard after each load was done. The sunshine and fresh breeze dried them quickly. When the boys went with me to get the cows for milking, Gertie Lou began ironing some of the cotton shirts.

I couldn't believe all the effort we had gone through to present an orderly house for Aunt Bertha. She must be a woman who demanded this family's respect. I guessed a clean house was the image that Mr. Wagner wanted to present to his older sister.

From what he had hinted, she would not be easily pleased, even though we had all worked hard. As Gertie Lou said, she was not used to children. So I planned to stay out of her way as best I could.

Chapter Twenty-Three

"Eddie, I'm taking some time off work this morning," Mr. Wagner said, as we finished up the milking. "I'm going to the bus station in New Richmond to pick up my sister Bertha. Then I'll bring her out here to the house. You get the kids up and have them eat their breakfast. Have Daniel help you get the cows back to the pasture when you're done eating. Today would be a good day to get the potatoes dug. The kids will help you with that."

Judging from the look on Mr. Wagner's face, I figured this was one bus he really wished he could miss. Maybe Aunt Bertha would change her mind if she really disliked visiting her brother and all his kids. I could always hope.

I brought two fresh pitchers of milk into the house and placed them in the refrigerator.

"Daniel... John... Wake up and get the kids up, too. Today Aunt Bertha is coming," I called upstairs.

No answer. I didn't even hear a tiny noise come from the upstairs bedrooms. I walked quietly up the steps and peeked in the boy's rooms. Pretending to be in deep sleep, the children were buried beneath their blankets.

"Hey, guys... I don't think you're sleeping," I said. "Let's go, you've gotta get up. This is Aunt Bertha day..."

"I know," Benjamin said with a giggle. "That's why we're hiding."

Then the blankets came off and everyone laughed along with Benjamin. It was funny now, but everyone knew that when Aunt Bertha arrived, life wasn't going to be a joke.

"Benjamin, you can set the bowls and spoons on the table," I said, as the children followed me downstairs to the kitchen.

"John, you get the cereal boxes, please, and grab some bananas out of the cupboard.

"Daniel, you put on the glasses and fill them with milk.

"Nathan, help James into his chair, and then you and Charles sit down while I get the twins in their high chairs. And get the girls bibs out of the drawer, too, please."

"I miss Mom," Benjamin said with sad, misty eyes.

"Mama too, Mama too," Elizabeth said.

Laura began hitting the table with her spoon as she did at most meals.

"Here Laura, let's put cereal in your dish," I said. "Now you can eat with your spoon."

"I know you all miss your mother. Maybe we'll hear how she is doing when your dad gets home," I said.

Our breakfast was interrupted with Chip's loud barking.

We heard a knock at the door, followed by a cheerful greeting.

"Hello. It's just me," Gertie Lou called, as she stuck her head in the door.

"Hi," I said. "Come in."

"Hi Gertie Lou," Benjamin said with a wide smile. He was joined by a chorus of other young greeters.

"I was driving by, so I stopped to see how you were doing,"

"Mr. Wagner is bringing Aunt Bertha out later after he picks her up at the bus," I said. "We're going to bring the cows back to the pasture now before he gets here."

"I'll read to the little ones while you go out to do that, if you like," Gertie said.

"Great. Come on, guys," I said to the older boys. "Let's get going before your aunt arrives."

"Here Chip," I called as I stepped outside. He came bounding right up to me. "Good Boy... Let's move these cows."

With Josie our lead cow heading down the driveway first, the others followed her, knowing that they were headed for the pasture land across the road. Chip navigated as best as a one-eyed dog could. His whole heart was back on duty as shepherd of this herd of cattle. As we approached the road, the more alert Chip appeared, sniffing the air, and he paused to listen for danger.

"Look, Eddie, my dad's car is coming down the road. Do you think he sees us?" John asked. "He'll soon be turning in the driveway. I hope he doesn't spook the cows."

"Keep them moving nice and easy. We can't stop them now," I said. "Go across and open the pasture gate."

"Dad sees us. He's stopping," John yelled as he ran across the road. Bring them over."

"Okay," I called to Daniel. "Let's move 'em out." Daniel continued to prod the cows on his side to hurry as fast as they could.

"Move, Josie...if you don't hurry, the rest won't either," I said.

Moments later, the last cow crossed the road and John shut the gate. I glanced quickly at the stern faced, non-smiling woman who sat in the passenger seat of Mr. Wagner's car as it approached us slowly.

"Got your morning chores done?" he asked through the open car window. I noticed his look was more sour than usual.

"Most everything, sir," I said.

"Then you can dig potatoes today. I've got to get back to work."

I nodded, and without further comment, he drove his sister up the long driveway to the farmhouse.

"Looks like we get to work outside, guys," I said. "Digging potatoes isn't such bad work. What do you think?"

"It's great. That job could keep us outside all day," Daniel said smiling.

"Yep," John agreed. "I'll be glad to help with anything that will keep me working as far away from Aunt Bertha as possible."

Chapter Twenty-Four

"Do we have to dig potatoes right now?" John asked.

"I don't know your Aunt Bertha, but it sounds like she might find jobs for us if we don't look busy," I said.

"She will," Daniel said. "Let's go dig the potatoes."

"Let's find all the outdoor stuff we can do," John said. "That way, she can't think up any jobs for us."

We were almost at the house when Gertie Lou came out of the back door. She climbed into her car and stopped for a moment on her way out the driveway.

"You boys remember to call me if you need anything," she said. "Here's my number, Eddie. Keep it in your pocket, just in case. Remember, Aunt Bertha doesn't know you children well. She might say things harshly, but I think she means well. I'm only a phone call away if you kids need to talk."

I wished Gertie Lou had come to stay with us and not Aunt Bertha. However, Gertie Lou had her own farm to run. Since her husband died, she managed their entire herd of beef cattle. Yet I knew, if we needed her, she would always be willing to help us.

"Boys, come up here to the house right now," Aunt Bertha yelled, as she stepped out on the porch. She was a fairly tall woman with her gray-blond hair drawn back in a bun. She wore glasses, which she adjusted frequently as she spoke.

"There you go, kids," Gertie Lou said. "You'd better answer her right away."

"Okay," I said.

Gertie Lou drove out the driveway with a wave and a comforting smile.

We walked up to the house. The children's stern, plain-faced aunt stood on the porch. She singled me out and looked me squarely in the eyes.

"So you're the foster kid."

She looked me up and down with a frown on her face, adjusting her glasses.

"I can't believe my brother would have taken in the likes of you…another skinny kid to feed. What can you do to earn your keep? You're one more hungry mouth at the table as far as I'm concerned."

She shook her head as though, in her eyes, I appeared an item of disgust. She wiped her hands on her apron, adjusted her glasses once again, and continued speaking.

"I've just received a phone call from your twin sister's social worker. She wants to set up a time for your sister and her foster parents to see you."

"Please, when are they coming?" I asked.

"They'll be here this afternoon about two o'clock," Aunt Bertha said.

"Today? Really?" I asked.

"That's what I said, didn't I?" Bertha replied with a scowl. "Now you and the big boys dig those potatoes that my brother wants out of the garden. Get started, so you'll get something accomplished before lunch. I always say, if you haven't worked up an appetite, you shouldn't bother to eat. Hurry up now."

Suddenly it didn't matter how Aunt Bertha insulted me. I would get to see Ellie again. I could meet her foster parents and know for sure if she was happy. I wanted to scream with excitement, but I didn't dare show my feelings.

Daniel and John looked at each other, and then at me, as we all three escaped to the tool shed before this drill sergeant of an aunt could give us any other orders.

"Daniel, you take this spade and grab that bushel basket over in the corner," I said. "John, you bring an armful of those gunny sacks hanging over there, and I'll bring the fork. When we dig we have to be careful not to poke holes in the potatoes. If we do, they'll start to rot."

"Do we have to wash all the potatoes right now?" John asked.

"No. We'll just brush the dirt off, and then we'll store them in gunny sacks in the root cellar. We'll wash them when we bring them up to the kitchen for our meals."

I remembered when I dug potatoes with Albert on the Schmidt farm. Mr. Schmidt's anger flared into an explosion if we stuck the fork tine into one potato. I could hear him shout and splatter us with horrid names. Poor Albert... I wondered how he was doing.

"Let's get to work," I said, and we headed toward the potato patch.

"See what we mean about our crabby Aunt Bertha?" John asked.

"Maybe we can get a lot of outside work done. What do you think?" I said with a grin. "We sure don't want to work with her inside the house."

We began to loosen the soil around the potato hills and carefully lifted out the large russet beauties that lay beneath the surface of the ground. After filling one sack, we heard a high screeching voice from the porch.

"John, you come up here and help Benjamin take care of these little brats. I can't get the twins to quit crying for their mother. I've never heard such a racket!" It seemed Aunt Bertha was loosing her grip on life at the Wagner farm, already.

"I don't want to go in that house with her yelling at the kids," John said.

"Go upstairs and get some books. Look at the pictures and tell the stories. You know them all by heart. And put Elizabeth and Laura on the floor right between you and Benjamin. Then they will feel safe. You can do that, John. If they quit crying, maybe Aunt Bertha will quit yelling."

John threw down the spade with a look of frustration.

"I'll do it for the little kids, but I sure don't know why she even has to be here. I knew it was going to be this way."

We dug and filled several more sacks of potatoes. Before we knew it, Aunt Bertha was out on the porch again.

"I'm serving lunch in five minutes," she yelled. "Come and get it, or go without. Makes no difference to me."

We tied our last sack with corn string and walked up to the house. After washing our hands at the sink, we pumped vigorously to rinse away the dirt and suds from the golden bar of soap, then we sat down at the table.

I looked for the usual stack of sliced bread for our lunch sandwiches, but found it missing. Instead, the table was set with plates and cups and silverware. I smelled a distinct odor of tuna in the air.

"We're having tuna hot dish for lunch today," Aunt Bertha announced. "I expect clean plates and no fussing about the menu."

This tuna hot dish was not like any other I had ever eaten. It wadded up like thick cement. Aunt Bertha blobbed each helping onto our plates with a large metal serving spoon.

"I thickened it up good so it would go further and stick to your bones," she added.

"But we don't like tuna," Benjamin said. "Especially the twins, they hate it."

"I figured that. So, I brought twelve cans with me when I came. It's a good food to have for tuna sandwiches, tuna salad, and tuna-cheese buns. You'll learn to like it when I'm through with you, or else you'll get good and hungry. That's for sure!"

I gulped down my food and thought of a silly saying I had heard from someone in my past: *'Over the teeth, over the gums, lookout stomach, here it comes.'* I finished my lunch off with an extra glass of milk. I excused myself from the table. Soon Daniel joined me in the potato patch.

"I can't believe her," Daniel complained. "How can we tolerate that mean woman in our family? Wait until my dad gets home. Then the trouble will fly into high gear. I've been thinking…what if we caught a snake and put it in her bed?"

"A snake? I think you boys would be in big trouble," I said with a laugh.

"Yeah, but think about it," Daniel said. "She would never know who did it. She'd be so scared, she'd pack her suitcase and leave. In fact, she might be mad enough to never come back. Maybe she'd never talk to my dad again."

As our conversation was getting interesting, Chip started to bark. He heard the sound of a car as it turned off the main road. I squinted hard against the sun, but I could see that it wasn't Gertie Lou or Mr. Wagner. A car I didn't recognize came slowly up the driveway.

Chapter Twenty-Five

As the car passed by the potato patch, I saw my twin sister Ellie wave. A young child sat next to her with her face pressed inquisitively against the window. The car parked in the driveway near the house. Finally, the time for the promised visit had arrived.

"That's my sister. I have to go now," I said to Daniel as I dropped the gunny sack right where I was standing.

I brushed my dusty hands on my pant legs and ran up the driveway. My emotions were strung tighter than a fiddle string. Ellie stepped out of the car and ran toward me with a big smile, her arms open to give me a hug. She was followed by a little girl who was determined not to let Ellie out of her sight.

"El-lie, El-lie, wait," the child called, her wobbly gait swinging her brown braids wildly back and forth.

"My El-lie," Emma said firmly, as she caught up to Ellie and forcefully took her hand.

"Hi, Ellie," I said, as I hugged my sister. "It's great to see you. But who's the little girl?"

"This is Emma. She is my whole life now. I'm a foster child in the home of Dr. Axel and Mrs. Meyers. Dr. Meyers is a dentist and his wife works in his office several hours a week doing bookwork. They have assigned me the job of being a companion to their daughter Emma.

"Emma was born with Downs Syndrome," Ellie explained. "It affects the way she learns, talks, and walks. She has no other siblings and wants to be with me all the time. I help her with all her personal needs. When school starts, I will walk with her to her special school before I go on to my school."

"Are you bored? I mean always trying to entertain her?" I asked.

"It's better than doing all those dishes and getting yelled at when we lived at the Schmidt farm. She's a sweet child. Her parents are kind, and they treat me well."

"Are you doing any cross-stitch projects?" I asked.

"Yes, I'm working on a tablecloth and napkins to match," Ellie answered. "I work on cross-stitch in the evening after Emma has gone to bed.

"After my school day, Emma's parents want me to get right home to be with her. She is dependent on me now. Her parents want to give her the best and they feel having a personal companion is what she really needs. But how are you doing, Eddie?"

"I get by. Mr. Wagner is a hard man like Mr. Schmidt, but he's gone a lot. Mrs. Wagner is a good mother. However, she is in the hospital right now. They have eight kids and I think they're going to have another baby, but something is wrong. She needs to rest a lot. Her husband brought her to the hospital three days ago. He hasn't told me or the older boys exactly what is happening, or when she can come home. The family has an aunt who came here to help out. She can't get along with the children, and the youngest ones keep crying for their mother. It's rough around here right now."

"El-lie, El-lie come," Emma said as she pulled on Ellie's arm.

"Yes, Emma," Ellie said. "Emma, this is my brother Eddie."

The child looked at me wonderingly, her blue eyes searching through her petite round spectacles.

I looked up toward the car. Ellie's foster parents stood watching our reunion. Evelyn Johnson, Ellie's kind social worker who made this visit possible, also gave me a brief wave as we walked toward the house. I recognized her warm compassionate look as she smiled at us. She made a promise to let Ellie visit me, and she kept it. I would always be grateful for that.

"Let's walk up to the car so I can introduce you to my foster parents," Ellie said.

"My El-lie," Emma said, as she continued to pull on Ellie's arm.

"It's okay, Emma," Ellie said, as she gave her a pat on the back. "We're only here for a short visit.

"Eddie, please meet Dr. Axel and Mrs. Meyers," Ellie said. "They are my foster parents now."

"Hi," I said as I shook the outstretched hand of this plump man with a wide smile. He was dressed in a classy tan suit and fancy white fedora hat.

"Good to meet you, son. We've certainly heard mighty good things about you. And this is my wife Adele," Dr. Meyers said.

"Hi," I said, as I shook Mrs. Meyer's hand. The slender dentist's wife had brown hair that curled gently around her face. Dressed in a fashionable brown suit and trendy tan hat to match, her blue eyes looked directly at me as she spoke.

"Hi, Eddie, we are very happy to meet our Ellie's brother. We think the world of her, and now meeting you is a real treat."

"Thank you," I said.

"I'm glad to see you again, Eddie," Mrs. Johnson said. "How are you doing?"

"Okay," I said. "I'll start school next week."

"Are you glad about that?"

"Yes," I said. "My foster mom is in the hospital so we have Mr. Wagner's sister staying here to help out."

"Oh," Mrs. Johnson said. "I hope things get back to normal for you and everyone else soon. I brought some cookies and lemonade. Would you like to sit down in the shade under those trees and have a snack? I have a blanket in my car for us to sit on."

Mrs. Johnson handed me the blanket and I spread it out on the ground. Little Emma helped, too, straightening her corner over and over.

I couldn't believe that the kind of cookies Mrs. Johnson baked were my favorite chocolate chips. They were absolutely the best. They reminded me of the chocolate chip cookies Mother Okerby used to bake for us when we lived with them...chock-full of chocolate chips, and the cookie was soft enough to melt in my mouth.

"Take some more Eddie," Mrs. Johnson said. "You look like you could use a few extra treats."

"Thank-you," I said as I felt my grin stretch from ear to ear.

As the adults settled into their own conversation, I had something I needed to tell Ellie.

"Remember the night Mrs. Fletcher left the farm?"

"I sure do. That was the horrible night that made them decide we needed to live with separate families."

"Something very strange happened on that evening that I didn't tell you about. I think you should know now, in case we don't see each other for a long time."

"I remember you stayed out in the barn for an extra long time that evening," Ellie said. "And I heard some noises in the kitchen before I went out to check on you."

"Well, here's the story: When I was finishing up in the barn, I saw someone jump off the train and run into the weeds by the train tracks. I searched in the long grass, and the other sheds. Finally, I decided to check up in the hay loft in the barn. I began climbing the ladder and called to see if someone was up there.

"A man's voice answered me and asked me to come up and help him. He was dressed in dirty old bib overalls and a faded engineer hat. Blood was seeping through on the sleeve of his torn blue-denim shirt. He said he scraped his arm when he jumped off the train.

"He told me he was awful hungry and thirsty, and he asked me to get him something to eat. The noise you heard in the kitchen was me making him a couple of roast beef sandwiches and a cream bucket of water."

"Eddie! You helped him? He could have been an escaped convict or bank robber. He could have hurt you."

"Wait…let me finish. The strange thing about it was that he knew my name and he knew about you, too. And look, he gave me this watch fob. His initials O. B. are carved into the leather. He said he sold his watch for food, but he wanted me to have this fob for helping him. Maybe someday I'll have my own watch to put on it."

"I still think it was a scary thing helping someone who jumped the train…you didn't have a clue what his motive was."

"Something about him made me feel like I'd seen him before. Maybe it was his eyes. And then when he knew my name and asked me if I had a twin sister living here, well, he seemed to have some connection with us, Ellie."

"I think we have to be careful about who we trust. We're on our own, and so many adults try to run our lives. I say we have to be really cautious."

"I know, Ellie. But I knew inside I needed to help him. I gave him a towel to wrap his bleeding arm, besides the food and water. It was the only right thing to do. In the morning when I went out to do the chores, he was gone. I suppose he jumped the next train and was on his way. I wonder if I'll ever see him again."

"It's just as well you didn't tell me that night. I would have been scared. I don't think I would have talked to him."

"I'm happy you are in a good home, now," I said. "Do you ever think about our other brothers and sisters? Mother and Father Okerby said there were other children in our family."

"Yes, I wonder about them, too. Where do you think they live? Where would we begin to look for them? I wouldn't know where to start. We haven't any idea how to get in touch with the Okerby family anymore, much less find our siblings."

"I know. I wondered if it ever crossed your mind, that's all. Maybe someday when we're older we'll find them."

The adult's conversation slowed and their attention turned to us once more.

"Well, kids, we've had a great visit, but it's time for us to leave," Mrs. Johnson said. "I'll pick up the picnic things while you twins say your goodbye."

"Emma, you come with Mama and Papa now," Mrs. Meyers took her daughter's hand and walked toward the car.

"No. I stay with El-lie. My El-lie," Emma began to cry and tried to pull away from her mother.

"Oh, my little lamb, you come to your Papa and let Ellie say a proper goodbye," Dr. Meyers said, and he picked up his fussing child. "Ellie will join us in a minute."

"I want my El-lie, my El-lie, my El-lieee," Emma wailed, as her father walked toward the car and climbed inside to join his wife and Mrs. Johnson.

"Wow, I guess you're loved," I said to Ellie as the cries continued from inside the car.

"I know she loves me, and she is a good little girl. But I do miss living in the same foster home with you, Eddie. I worry that the welfare won't tell me if they move you away from this place. Then I'll never know where you're living."

"No, I don't trust them to tell us the truth. I guess the only reason you got to come today is because Mrs. Johnson made us that promise on the day we were separated. We have to remember what Mother Okerby told us when we left their home: *Remember, God is with you wherever you go, and He hears your prayer.*"

"Yes, thanks for reminding me of that. I'm glad you're my brother," Ellie said with trickles of tears running down her cheeks. "Maybe, someday when we're on our own, we'll find each other."

I gave my sister a hug and watched her walk toward the car to join her foster family. Chip came up to me and stood wagging his tail as I watched Mrs. Johnson's car go back down the driveway. Emptiness drained into the lonely hole in my heart as Ellie left my life once again.

Chapter Twenty-Six

I walked slowly toward the potato patch to join Daniel. The sadness I felt at seeing Ellie leave took away my ambition.

"Eddie, come here quick. Look what I found," Daniel said as he stood by the bushel basket with a gunny sack tied tightly with corn string.

"What?" I said as I noticed the gunny sack in a writhing motion.

"Be ready to look quick cause I can only open it for a fast peek."

"Are you serious about your snake idea?" I asked.

"I sure am! We gotta do something. Aunt Bertha won't even let the little kids outside to play. It's a nice day, and they're stuck in the house where she can watch them."

"You sure got a good one," I said with a grin. "But your dad will be angry."

"He'll be glad to get her out of here, too," Daniel said.

"I'll probably be the one that will get blamed. I don't think you should do this," I said. "She'll be crazy mad at all of us if she finds out someone put it in her bed."

"I'm hiding it in the barn and then tonight I'm going to put it in her bed," Daniel said.

I could tell he had made up his mind. I could advise against this plan all I wanted, but I was sure he wouldn't listen.

"We have to get the cows up to the barn for milking now, so let's go get John," I said. "Maybe you'd better not include him in your little plan. Something tells me that if things go wrong, he might tell on you. Then you'd be in big trouble."

"Don't worry. I wasn't planning to tell anyone but you. If it works out, it's our secret. If it doesn't work, at least we tried."

* * *

"Everyone get your hands washed and go to the table," Aunt Bertha said. "We're going to start eating. Your father should be home soon."

"What are we having for supper?" Benjamin asked.

"It's my wonderful seven bean soup, with cauliflower creamed sauce. I threw in the left over tuna hot dish from lunch, too. I have a saying: Throw it out…go without…so I use up all the leftovers."

"But we give our leftovers to Chip," Benjamin said.

"You are a snippy little kid if I ever heard one," Aunt Bertha snapped. "I've heard about enough out of the likes of you, young man."

Benjamin dropped his head and gave his aunt no further suggestions about the meal.

As at every meal, Laura began to drum on her high chair tray with her spoon.

Bang, bang, bang, bang.

"Stop that child!" Aunt Bertha yelled. "I can't take all this noise."

I reached over and gave Elizabeth and Laura each a small piece of bread. Elizabeth smiled and Laura stopped drumming as they chewed the bread pieces contentedly.

I looked at Daniel, who scowled at Aunt Bertha's comment. Maybe Daniel was right. This woman was a disruption to the whole family.

"John, get the pitcher of milk and pour each of us a glass. I'll fill the bowls with soup," Aunt Bertha ordered.

She scooped large portions of her odd smelling soup into our bowls. I decided it would be safer to eat it while it was hot, so I gulped it down with two slices of bread and butter and three glasses of milk.

As I was draining my last glass of milk, Mr. Wagner walked through the door.

"It's about time you get home and help me with this bunch of wild urchins you're raising out here in the country," Aunt Bertha said. "I can't believe how your Missus puts up with them all. The young ones have cried all day long to go outside. I told them "No." I can't keep an eye on them out there." She stopped to take a breath and shove her glasses up on her nose.

"Then this foster kid had company all afternoon. His twin sister visited. The social worker said I had to let them see each other before school. So he and Daniel didn't finish digging all of the potatoes."

"Just a minute, Bertha. If it's too much for you, why don't you leave?" Mr. Wagner said in an angry tone. "My kids are used to playing outside everyday when it isn't pouring rain. No wonder they fussed if you kept them trapped inside here with the likes of you."

"Yeah, that's just like it. Stick up for your bratty kids. That's why they don't behave. There's no discipline in this house. No respect for their elders."

"Oh Bertha, I might have known it wouldn't work to have you come," Mr. Wagner said. "You and I have never seen eye to eye since we were kids. It's no use. Pack up your things and I'll drive you back to your house. I've got a neighbor that will help out until Janet gets on her feet. We'll make it just fine."

"If I walk out that door, you'll be sorry! I won't even be back for Christmas. You live like a pack of rats out here. I've seen all I want to see of you or your kids for a good long time," Bertha said with a sneer.

"Well, that goes for us too, Bertha," Mr. Wagner shouted. "Get your stuff ready and I'll drive you back tonight, after we milk those blessed cows."

We all sat speechless after this tirade took place. One by one we cleared our dishes and left the table. John and Daniel followed me out to the barn.

"Hey Daniel, guess you won't need the encouragement in the gunny sack, will you?" I said. "You can let that poor little critter go."

"Yeah, I'm going to do that right now. Poor snake. He might have been as scared of Aunt Bertha as she was of him, if we would have gone through with it. Imagine how loud she would have hollered!"

"At least she's leaving. When my mom comes home, she won't have to listen to the mean things Aunt Bertha says about our family," Daniel said.

Mr. Wagner entered the barn with a dark, angry look.

"Let's see if we can get this milking done in record time," he said. "I want to get this woman back to her house as soon as possible…even if I drive all night."

"Dad, when are you going to tell us about Mom? Is she coming home soon?" John asked.

"We are going to have another baby at our house," he said. "But Mom needs rest right now, and the doctor wants to do some tests to make certain the baby is okay. When Mom comes home, she is going to need lots of help."

"We can help. We don't need Aunt Bertha to stay with us anymore, Dad," Daniel said. "It was bad having her here. She hates us, you know."

"It seems that way to hear her talk. I should never have asked her to come in the first place," Mr. Wagner said. "We'll get along."

"Mr. Wagner," I said. "Gertie Lou gave me her phone number if we needed to call her."

"She did? That was mighty neighborly of her," Mr. Wagner said. "She's been a good friend for years. We didn't want to take advantage of her. But if she said you kids could call, I'll let her know what's happening. Maybe she can help us out with the wash and the other things you kids can't do alone. I might as well pay her as anyone else."

After nearly an hour passed, I looked out the barn door and saw a sullen Aunt Bertha sitting bitterly in the car waiting for her ride back to civilization. She looked straight ahead through her glasses, that once again had slipped down on her nose. Her angry look gave no hint of remorse for her unkind words to this family.

Chapter Twenty-Seven

The day after Labor Day meant the first day of school. Mrs. Wagner was still in the hospital, so it was up to us to get ready on our own. After Aunt Bertha left, a peaceful calm settled over the household. Even Mr. Wagner's attitude seemed lighter. But I wondered how long that would last.

"Gertie Lou will come over and stay with you little kids, when the older kids leave for school," he said at breakfast. "I have to get to work, but I'm bringing Mom home from the hospital this afternoon.

"Is she well enough to stay home?" Benjamin asked.

"I hope so," his father said. "She needs to rest a lot, so you kids will have to help. Gertie Lou will prepare meals for us to heat up.

"You boys know how to pack lunches for school. Each of you choose a lunch pail and make a peanut butter sandwich. There are apples in the cupboard for your lunches, too."

"Mom loves flowers," Benjamin said. "I'm picking her a bouquet of those bright yellow ones by the driveway. I have to get a quart jar for a vase."

Donald Wagner sighed as he watched his son run down to the cellar where the canning jars were stored.

"I'm leaving for work," the children's father said, as he grabbed his lunch pail. He turned to walk out the door, and we all heard Chip bark and growl in ferocious, guttural tones.

I went to the window to see Chip standing near the long grass by the side of the driveway. A sickly looking skunk was making his way out of the grass, walking toward the house.

"We got a sick varmint out here," Mr. Wagner said, as he came back in the kitchen. "I'm going to put him out of his misery. When a skunk comes walking in the daylight like this, it could be rabid."

"Can we go watch, Dad?" John asked.

"Better not. You never know where a skunk like that can spray. It's a putrid smell. You look in the window."

Chip barked franticly as he inched toward the intruder. Yet the skunk persisted in the direction of the house. Armed with his shotgun, Donald Wagner stepped out on the porch, took aim, and put him down with his first shot.

The muggy September air lay heavy with nasty fumes. The odor penetrated through the crack in the back door. We could smell it inside the kitchen. Poor Chip could hardly abide the aroma as he rolled in the grass on the far side of the lawn, trying to rid himself of the stench.

"Eddie, I've got to get to work," my foster father said to me. He had come back into the house to put his shotgun away. "Take a pitchfork and throw that dead skunk out in the manure pile before you go to school."

"Okay," I answered. Yuk, I thought. I wish I didn't have to touch that putrid thing. But we certainly couldn't leave it where it was.

After getting rid of the blood-soaked critter, I ran down to the basement and got three quarts of tomato juice. I remembered that one of my friends in 4-H told me they used tomato juice to take away the smell from their dog who fought with a skunk. I also filled a five gallon pail of water.

"Daniel, come and help me for a minute," I called.

"What do you want?" Daniel asked.

"Hold Chip still for me," I said.

"What are you doing?"

"You watch and see," I said as I rubbed tomato juice into Chip's stinky coat. The poor dog smelled so bad it made my eyes water. As I rubbed in the juice, I could tell the scent was beginning to lift.

"It's okay, Chip. You're going to smell like a dog again. Not like a skunk, or a tomato," I said.

"I never heard of this treatment," Daniel said. "I'm glad you could think of something to do. I'd hate to just leave him like this. He doesn't like the way he smells either."

"A friend of mine used it on his dog, and he said that it really worked. Now we have to rinse the tomato juice out. But we'll need at least two more buckets of water."

After the rinse, Daniel let Chip go and he shook himself again and again, then he rolled over and over in the fresh, clean grass. The skunk scent was mostly all gone from his coat.

"Now let's get those cows back in the pasture and get ready for school," I said.

As I spoke, Gertie Lou drove up in our driveway.

"Hi boys," she said. "Are you ready for the first day of school?"

"Not exactly," I said. "We have to bring the cattle back to the pasture and we still haven't made our lunches."

"I can get the lunches ready," Gertie Lou answered. "You hurry on with the cows and your lunch pails will be done when you get back. Then you can get washed up, change clothes, and leave for school. By the way, it smells like skunk over on the other side of the driveway. Did you see a skunk around here?"

"We've had quite a morning. We'll tell you about it when we get back to the house. Right now we'd better get these cows back to pasture," I said. "I don't want to be late on the first day with a new teacher."

Chapter Twenty-Eight

"Thanks for packing our lunches," I told Gertie Lou.

"You're welcome. I put in some fresh chocolate chip cookies for each of you," she said with a smile..

"Who picked these beautiful Brown-eyed Susan's?" Gertie Lou asked.

"I picked them for my mom," Benjamin said with a wide grin. "She's coming home tonight."

"Your mom is going to love them. What a nice bright welcome home surprise. You are so thoughtful. This is your first day of school, isn't it, Benjamin?"

"Yes," he said as his smile dissolved into a serious look.

"Are you excited?" Gertie Lou asked.

"Sort of… I'm kind of scared. I wish my mom was home this morning."

"Tomorrow she will be here. That will help, won't it?" she asked.

Benjamin nodded soberly.

It was my first day at this new school, too. I had a queasy stomach and felt nervous, like I always did on all first days.

We hurried to wash off any remaining skunk smell and changed into our school clothes. I put on socks and my black school shoes that Mrs. Wagner and I had purchased at Swanson's Family Shoe Store. They felt awkward and heavy after I had gone barefoot all summer. But I knew they were the right size because I had seen my feet in that machine.

Weeks ago, Mrs. Wagner had purchased tablets and pencils for us on one of her trips to town, too. She had stored them safely in the top drawer of the buffet waiting for this day.

"Don't forget your school supplies," John reminded us.

Benjamin hurried to grab his tablet and pencil from the drawer, leaving one tablet and a pencil for me. The wide-ruled tablets had red covers and advertised Johnson's Variety Store in town. I grabbed the last pencil, picked up my dinner pail, and hurried to the door.

"Let's get going, guys. We've got a mile to walk," I said as we headed out the door.

Meadowlarks sang. We hustled along the road on this bright fall morning. A red-winged black bird swooped down past our troop, and butterflies darted about lighting here and there. I longed for some of their freedom to follow my dream, too. I wanted to explore who I really am. Where did I come from before Ellie and I landed in the Okerby family? I had many questions, but few answers.

Sometimes it bugged me not to have answers. Then again, I put it out of my mind. When I am an adult, I will investigate those words Father Okerby said to us: *We learned that the twins own mother had become ill and could not care for them…their father had no work, a sick wife, twin babies, and eight other children."*

What he said meant I have siblings out in the world somewhere. Someday I'm going to find them.

"We're almost at school, Benjamin," Daniel said. "Are your legs tired?"

"I'm doing okay," he said. "But maybe tomorrow we should start earlier so we don't have to walk so fast."

We soon came to the small white schoolhouse. The United

States flag fastened securely to the top of a strong metal flag pole, waved against the blue sky. I noticed a ramp built next to the stairway into this school building.

As the children gathered, they took turns playing on the swings, the teeter-totter, and the slippery slide. Everyone waited for the teacher to ring the bell that would call us inside for our school day to begin.

"I want to swing on the high swing," Benjamin said.

He hurried to squeeze in line for a turn, but at that moment, the teacher rang her hand bell. I saw a disappointed look on his face and grinned remembering how I felt when I was in first grade, too.

We began walking toward the stairway when a black car drove up into the school yard. I heard a girl standing behind me say in a loud voice to several other girls:

"Look, Jesse's finally here." The girl ran toward the car and called excitedly: "Hey, I thought you were going to be late. Hurry up so we all can sit together."

"I'm sorry, but I had to make one more trip to the barn to check my rabbit's cage. Miss Abigail's due to have her babies any time, and I can hardly wait!"

"Thanks, Dad," she said to her father, as he lifted her wheelchair out of the car.

"Have a good day at school, honey," her father said, as this smiling young girl eased into her wheelchair. "I promise I'll keep an eye on Miss Abigail for you." He gave her a pat on her shoulder, got back into his car, and drove out of the schoolyard.

"Well c'mon, let's go, Amy," Jesse said, as she whipped her wheelchair around and rolled it up the ramp with the help of her friend. The other girls came up to join them, and they all entered the school building.

I was amazed. I recognized Jesse as the energetic, determined girl I had met a year ago. She came and talked to me when I was showing Half-Pint, my calf, at the St. Croix County Fair. Way back then she told me she wanted to have an animal project of her own. Now, by what I've overheard, it sounds like she's achieved that dream.

I'm happy for her and I'd like to tell her, but so far she hasn't recognized me. Maybe I can talk to her later, I thought.

"Good Morning, class. My name is Miss Agnes Reed. Welcome to our first day of school," our stern looking teacher said, as she looked over her class. "Please find a desk. It's time we start our day." She spoke in a commanding voice and her piercing brown eyes scanned the classroom, observing each student's movement.

She was a short woman with black hair slightly waved in front and drawn back into a bun. When she looked at me, her dark eyes seemed to know what I was thinking. Black rimmed glasses hung on a chain around her neck. She wore a brown skirt and a tan blouse with a cameo broach. Her low heeled sturdy brown shoes did not add to her height. I wondered if she was even shorter than some of the older students.

The younger children quickly found places to sit in the smaller desks in front, followed by the older students filling in behind them. Amy, Jessie, and their friends chose desks next to each other. The year seemed off to a good start for them.

After finding my desk, I sat down and looked around the schoolroom. In front were blackboards. Stretched above them, was tacked a boarder of upper and lower case letters of the alphabet. That's handy for the first graders learning to print, I thought.

The teacher's desk and captain style chair also sat up in front. On the wall to the teacher's right side, stood a large globe on a metal stand that could spin around for viewing any country. I could tell this because one older student walked by and gave it a good whirl on the way to finding his desk.

I saw what appeared to be a large map rack on the opposite wall and a large picture of George Washington, hung beside it. Also against this wall stood an older upright piano, with the flag of the United States of America at its side.

Off to the right of the main classroom, a door marked "Library" led to the school's collection of reading material. A brightly colored poster hung on a bulletin board near that door, describing new library books that would be arriving soon.

The boys and girls cloak rooms were at the back of the main classroom. Hooks on the wall provided a place to hang a jacket or coat. Shelves for lunch pails and extra personal belongings hung above the hooks.

I noticed the sign: RESTROOMS. A school with indoor bathrooms was not like my other country school. An indoor bathroom at school seemed like a luxury.

"Please sit down," Miss Reed spoke curtly to the students who seemed to want to talk to their friends. "Our class will come to order." The tone of her voice overpowered her height, and for the moment, Apple River School became silent.

Chapter Twenty-Nine

"We will begin each morning by saying the pledge of allegiance to our flag. Each day, I will choose a different flag monitor. Today I will ask Benjamin Wagner to do this job."

I watched Benjamin get out of his seat and walk slowly toward the teacher. "You may stand right next to the American flag, Benjamin, and please lead us in the pledge. If you don't know all the words, I will help you."

I placed my hand over my heart and began, "*I pledge allegiance to the flag...*" As I continued reciting the words, I noticed how pleased Benjamin looked that he had been chosen for this special job. I was proud of him. He certainly didn't act like a shy baby on his first day of school.

"Each day following the Pledge, we will sing a patriotic song. Today we will sing, *America*," Miss Reed said. "Do we have a class member that plays the piano?" I noticed that Jessie's friend Amy raised her hand. "Amy, would you like to play this song for the class when we sing?" Miss Reed asked.

"Yes, I'll try," Amy said.

"I have the music in the *Golden Book of Favorite Songs* here on the piano. We will just sing the first verse for today," Miss Reed said.

Amy left her desk and walked toward the piano. She adjusted the bench, sat down, and brushed her dark curls away from her cheeks. As she gave us the starting chord, the class began to sing:

"My country 'tis of thee, Sweet land of liberty…" with Miss Reed's strong voice in the lead.

"Thank you, Benjamin and Amy," Miss Reed said as we finished. "Our school piano is terribly out of tune. I promise we will get a piano tuner in here soon.

"This is my first year teaching at Apple River School," Miss Reed said, as she walked back and forth in front of the class. "I am asking each of you to give your name and then tell the class something that you like to do. That will help us all get to know each other. We'll begin in the front row with Benjamin."

"My name is Benjamin Wagner and I like to play with my dog Chip. I'm trying to train him to fetch."

"Great, Benjamin," Miss Reed said. "Caring for a pet teaches responsibility. We will be having a special pet project in just a few weeks. Maybe Chip could come to school for a visit on that day."

Benjamin nodded with a grin.

A little girl that sat in the seat across from Benjamin had long brown braids. She seemed bashful and spoke softly with her head bowed down. "My name is Audrey "Th"-wingly, and I love "th"-inging."

"Speak up, Audrey, so we can all hear you," Miss Reed said. "Singing is wonderful and we will be singing a lot in our school this year." The little first grader with a lisp lifted her head up a tiny bit and allowed a quick smile in return.

Another first grader with a long black pony tail and big brown eyes sat in the next row in the front seat. "I'm Rosemarie Ellis. I like to draw with colored art pencils."

"I'm certain you will have many opportunities to draw in our school," Miss Reed said.

Rosemarie smiled.

Other students gave their names and soon it was Daniel's turn to speak. "My name is Daniel Wagner. I love to work with the cattle on my dad's farm…especially raising the young calves. I'd like to have a farm of my own someday."

I thought it was amazing that a kid who worked so hard on a farm still dreamed of being a farmer as an adult.

"It's good to have a goal to work toward early in life," Miss Reed said. "You seem to be a young man that is not afraid of hard work. A good farmer needs to study hard in school. I hope you will become an excellent student on your way to owning your farm."

"My name is John Wagner and I love to read."

"Reading can be a life-long pastime," the teacher said. "You will never be bored if you learn to read well and have a good book available. We are enlarging our library this year. You will find new books to enjoy. In fact, I am going to hold a "Reader's Raceway Contest." Our new books will be delivered within the week and the contest will begin in two weeks. I'll be announcing the rules and prizes when the new books arrive."

"My name is Jessie Baxter. I love raising my rabbits for 4-H, especially my doe rabbit, Miss Abigail and my buck, Mr. Moses. They are so tame and anyone can hold them. I raise them for selling as pets.

"That's interesting, Jessie," Miss Reed said. "Do you suppose you could bring your rabbits for the pet project?"

"I think so…if my dad is available to help me transport them," Jessie said. I could sense by the tone of excitement in her voice that she must enjoy 4-H the same way I did when I raised my 4-H calf Half-Pint.

"My name is Amy Hall. I enjoy playing the piano. I've only taken lessons for two years so I'm still learning." Her dark curly hair bounced as she talked and smiled.

"Yes, and you play well. How wonderful to have a student musician in our classroom," Miss Reed said. "When our school piano gets tuned correctly, you will enjoy playing for future classroom music events."

"My name is Edgar Granlund. I love to play ball. I hope we can get some games going at recess time."

"Well, Edgar, Let's put you in charge of getting the recess ball teams started. Make certain to include everyone that would like to play. Will you do that for us?"

"Yes, ma'am."

"My name's Sid Jones. I moved to my Grandpa's farm three weeks ago. I used to live in Minneapolis before my dad died."

I noticed that this was the student with the matted brown hair that sent the globe in a spin as he walked to find a desk. As he talked, he poked at his desk top with his lead pencil slowly carving an image into the wood.

"What are your hobbies or something you enjoy, Sid?" Miss Reed asked.

"I don't have no hobbies, and I hate living out here in the country. I moved away from all my friends in the city and I'm going back as soon as my mom can save enough to send for me."

"Welcome to Wisconsin, Sidney. I hope you'll make new friends while you live here, even if it is for a short while. "Now if you... Yes, Sidney? Did you raise your hand?"

"I'm Sid, not Sidney. I hate the name, Sidney," he said with a glare.

"I'll call you Sid if you wish, but I'd appreciate if you would quit writing on your desk top."

Sid's eyes turned away as he slammed his pencil down. But his rebellious look washed over his face in a dark scowl.

Finally, I was the last student to speak. "My name is Eddie Brewster. I raised a Holstein calf named Half-Pint for 4-H. I don't have him anymore, but it was the best thing I ever did. I guess I really love all animals. Someday I'd like to have a dog of my own."

"That's great, Eddie. I hope you'll see that dream through and become a pet owner yourself."

I wish I could tell this teacher that it was impossible for me to dream about owning my own dog. A foster kid like me can't depend on being in one place long enough to keep a pet. If I got a dog, I might get good and used to having him. Then one day when I'd least expect it, a car will drive up and a social worker will say: "Eddie, pack up your box. You're moving to a different family, but you can't take your dog." That would really hurt. No, it's better not to get attached.

Chapter Thirty

"How did you like school, Benjamin?" I asked, as I watched him trudge along, trying to keep up with his brothers.

"It's okay," he said grinning. "I'm gonna tell Mom I got to be flag monitor."

"Yeah, and you did a good job, too," I said. "She'll be proud of you."

John and Daniel ran on ahead, but I knew that a long chore list waited for us when we reached the farm. I didn't mind being the one to walk a little slower with Benjamin.

"Hey Eddie," Benjamin said, as he bent over beside the road, "Look at this rock. I think it's an agate." Benjamin was always on the look-out for interesting rocks. He arranged the best ones in his mother's flower garden.

"You're right. This is an agate, Benjamin. You've got good eyes," I said, as I handed his latest find back to him.

"Thanks," he said and shoved it into his pant's pocket.

As we reached the driveway, I noticed both Gertie Lou and the Wagner cars were parked by the house. Was Mrs. Wagner home from the hospital?

"Dad's car is home, Eddie," Benjamin said. "Let's go find out what's happening."

"Okay. I'll race you."

Chip bounded down the driveway to meet us. He must have

missed us on this first day of school, as he barked loudly and wagged his tail. He turned and playfully ran along side us as we hurried up to the house.

When we walked in the door, Mrs. Wagner was lying on the couch in the living room, with Gertie Lou sitting beside her in the rocker. She looked pale and tired, but when she saw her children, a warm smile swept over her face.

"Oh kids, come over here where I can take a good look at you." She hugged her three boys. "I've missed you terribly. It seems like I've been gone such a long time."

"Oh hello, Eddie," my foster mom said, as though I was an afterthought. There it was! The foster kid. I didn't quite fit into a family situation again.

"Hi, kids," Gertie Lou greeted us warmly.

"How was school?" the children's mother asked.

"Okay," Daniel answered. "We've got a strict teacher, though. She's not much taller than Eddie."

"What's her name?"

"Miss Reed," John answered. "She wanted to know stuff about everybody, because she's new around here."

"Yeah, I told her about Chip," Benjamin said with a grin.

"That's good," Janet Wagner said. "We have something to talk to you older kids about before the little ones wake up from their nap. The reason I have been feeling so tired lately is that we are going to have another baby in our house. I've had some physical problems this time causing me to need treatment in the hospital for these past weeks."

"Are you okay now, Mom?" Benjamin asked with a serious look.

"Well, from now on until the baby comes, I must have lots of rest. You will need to be my good helpers and do my running for me. Can you do that?"

"Of course we can, Mom," Daniel said in a most grown-up manner. "But you will need to tell us what to do."

"I'll help the best I can," Benjamin said. "I'm really growing up fast, Mom. You can count on me. I even got to be flag monitor at school today."

"Benjamin, that's wonderful, I'm proud of you," his mother said. "What does the flag monitor do?"

"He or she has to stand up by the flag and lead the class in reciting the Pledge of Allegiance. I didn't know all the words, but the teacher helped me."

"We can practice it so every one of you will memorize it. Someday you will each have a turn to be flag monitor, I'm sure. And where did this bouquet of beautiful Brown-eyed Susan's come from?"

"I picked them for you," Benjamin said with a grin.

"Thank you, honey. What a welcome home present. They brightened this whole room."

"Mom, when is the baby going to come?" John asked with an unusually serious tone in his voice.

"Some time around Thanksgiving... Won't that be exciting? But the doctor has warned me that I must rest so our baby will be healthy. We have hired Gertie Lou to help when she can, and Eddie is a strong boy. You must listen to his advice and help him with the chores without arguing. We will all do our best."

I noticed that Mr. Wagner said nothing. He stood in the kitchen gazing out the window. I couldn't understand the dark, sober look on his face, while his wife explained such exciting news to the children.

"Eddie," he said in a gruff voice as he entered the living room, "You boys bring the cows up from the pasture for milking. We've got to get going on our chores."

"I'll be on my way home now," Gertie Lou said quickly. "I'm

glad you're home with your family, Janet. Call me when you need something. I've got a hot dish for your supper in the fridge. Also, some sliced tomatoes and cucumbers. Have Eddie put the hot dish in the oven before he gets the cows."

She turned and gave me an understanding look. Somehow I think she knew that I was beginning to feel that I had a lot of orders to fill.

I put the food in the oven and joined the boys, who were outside ready to bring the cows to the barn. Hard working Chip trotted along beside us as we hurried down the driveway to get the cattle.

"Eddie, look…over in the corner of the pasture," John said as we approached the gate. "It looks like we've got a cow down."

"You're right. Let's go find out what's wrong."

As we approached, a few black crows flew up off the carcass of one of the Wagner's older cows.

"It's Millie," Daniel said, as he ran ahead to check out the problem. "She's dead, and those dang birds are already trying to pick at her."

The birds settled on the ground several yards away. I guessed that Millie had not been dead for more than a few hours, but these creatures were determined to claim their rights to her carcass. The intense look in their eyes watched our every move, waiting for the chance to fly back in and continue their feast.

I could see Millie's stomach was terribly bloated. I knew something was wrong.

"There's a hole in the fence over here," Daniel said. "She must have pushed her way into some of this new clover. My dad says eating too much of that stuff when it's wet can make a cow good and sick. That's probably why her belly is swelled up like that."

"Let's go get the rest of the cows, and then we'll tell your dad," I said. "He'll want to check this out right away."

Chapter Thirty-One

"Let's eat. Then we can get the cows milked," Mr. Wagner said, after he had gone to the pasture to tend to Millie. His cheerless attitude ruined our welcome-home supper for his wife.

"Now we've got a dead cow and a hole in the fence to worry about, too." he said. "I've called the rendering service to haul her out of here. That's more money gone down the drain. If only she hadn't busted into that dang wet clover this morning. A cow can get fearful gas and indigestion from eating that rich wet stuff. She'll bloat up like a balloon. If there's no one was around to tap her, she's a goner."

"What do you mean 'tap her,' Dad?" Benjamin asked.

"You have to stick the cow with a sharp tool of some sort and slip in a tube to let the gas out. The veterinarian has a special instrument. I use a thin blade of a knife. If you don't get to her soon enough, she suffocates and dies."

Donald Wagner heaped the hamburger and tomato hot dish onto his plate and reached for two slices of bread, which he slathered with butter, and slapped together sandwich style. "Benjamin, pass those tomatoes and cucumbers this way," his father said.

"Here, Dad," Benjamin said. He slid the plate along the table.

"Daniel, get some more milk, the pitcher's nearly empty," Mr. Wagner ordered, as he gulped down his milk to the last drop in his glass.

My foster mother called from her bed on the couch. "Boys, are you helping Elizabeth and Laura finish their supper? I'm nearly done with my tray. I'm going to get up and walk out to the outhouse. I'll take the girls with me, if they need to go."

I helped the twins out of their high chairs.

"Do you want to go to the potty with your mom?" I asked.

"Me go potty," Elizabeth said.

"Me, too," Laura agreed, as both girls took their mother's hands and walked out the back door. Mrs. Wagner's patient attitude continued through her husband's grumbling. She did as much as she could to help with the children, and she seemed genuinely happy to be home.

"Eddie, I'm going out to get the fence repaired. You get this supper mess cleaned up and then head out to the barn to milk," Mr. Wagner commanded. "John, you help Eddie. Daniel, you come with me and get started milking."

I noticed the boys didn't waste time following their father's orders when he was in this mood, so I moved in a hurry, too. Refusal to do as he asked would not be a good idea.

We finished up in the kitchen and walked toward the barn when the black rendering truck pulled into the yard. The round faced driver stuck his head out of the window. "Hey kid," he said to me, as he pushed his cap up onto his wide forehead with his grimy hand. "You know where the dead cow's at?"

"One minute and I'll get Mr. Wagner."

In a few moments, the truck headed toward the pasture, led by Mr. Wagner's car filled with fencing materials. Millie's carcass would soon be gone, and the hole in the fence would be fixed.

* * *

That night as I tried to sleep, I heard the voice of my foster father continuing to complain about his worrisome financial state. "Right now I can't decide if it's worth it to have him around. He's another mouth to feed. It won't be long and I'll be laid off my construction work. There won't be many jobs after freeze up. Then I can do more here on the farm."

"What do you mean? You'd actually give up the welfare check and Eddie's help here?" Mrs. Wagner's voice sounded troubled. "He does so much for us all. He's become like a part of the family."

"Now there's where you're wrong," I heard Donald Wagner's coarse reply. "We got eight kids, and one on the way. We aren't about to claim any foster kid as part of our family. It's time to move him along if you're getting that attached."

I felt sick...that same pain in my stomach that I couldn't describe to anyone. A stab wound couldn't hurt as much as not belonging.

"Donald, we have to think of what is best for everyone. I don't think letting him move out is a good thing when I'm supposed to be on bed rest with this baby. We can use that money from the welfare."

"I'm sick and tired of talking about money. There's a hospital bill I can't pay. I struggle to buy groceries for this family, and my work is never done. I can't handle it, Janet. I can't handle it."

"But Donald... Eddie's here to help us and he works hard."

Then the talking stopped.

I heard footsteps stomp loudly, and the screen door slam shut. The car ignition popped, and the engine raced. I got out of my bed and looked out the upstairs window. I watched as Mr. Wagner's car sped out the driveway.

Chapter Thirty-Two

I crawled back into my bed. Will I have to move again? I tried to put their conversation out of my mind, but I couldn't sleep.

Somewhere deep in the night, I heard the sound of a car in the driveway. I listened for footsteps on the porch, and then I heard the kitchen door close. I got up and stood in the dark at the top of the stairs. This time I heard only whispers. I went back to my bed and drifted off to sleep.

Several weeks of school passed. The warmth of summer disappeared into an early fall chill. We hustled to get our morning chores done in time for school.

"Hey Eddie, do you remember that this is pet day?" Benjamin asked. "I have to get Chip ready to go with us this morning."

"Yes, I know. You've told me three times this week."

"Well, it's important that I brush Chip one more time."

"I know. I'm almost done feeding the calves. You go brush Chip, change into your school clothes, and eat your breakfast."

I finished my work and walked toward the house. Into the driveway drove Gertie Lou.

"Hi, Eddie," she called. "You kids want a ride to school? This is pet day, isn't it?"

"Yes. Benjamin would like that. He's worried about Chip walking the whole way to school. He's afraid he might chase off after a rabbit."

"I thought so. You go get changed and I'll give you a ride."

* * *

When we entered our schoolroom, pets of all different sizes and shapes had come for a visit.

As usual, Miss Reed made this event an opportunity for education as well as for entertainment. She gave note cards to the students. On these cards they were to write one thing they had learned from pet ownership and place it on their cage, or container.

"Hi Jesse," I said as I saw my friend adjusting the bedding in her rabbit's cage. "Is this your famous 'Miss Abigail'?"

"That's right," she said with a grin. "She's pretty special to me."

I was glad Jesse and I could be class mates and renew our friendship that began over a year ago, at the county fair. "Can I do anything to help?" I offered.

"I could use someone to fill the water bottles in these cages. Dad had to leave for work, so he didn't have time to do it. These are my other rabbits, 'Pokey' and 'Mr. Moses.'"

"I'd be glad to get them water," I said. It felt good to have a part in this pet exhibit, even though I had no pet of my own to show.

"Eddie," Benjamin said. "What can I use for a leash? The other dogs all have a leash."

"How about having Chip sit next to you without a leash, like he does at home?" I asked. "He does what you tell him to."

"I guess I can try. But I hope he doesn't run after Jessie's rabbits."

"If Miss Reed says anything, tell her Chip isn't used to a leash."

Benjamin walked back to his seat and Chip sat quietly beside him. But only for a moment…suddenly, Chip spotted Audrey

Swingley walking toward the exhibit table with a white metal bird cage swaying gently in her upraised hand. Chip immediately felt the need to bark a loud warning to everyone of this unusual moving metal object.

Audrey's bright yellow canary darted back and forth on its perch and flew into a tizzy. He flapped his wings wildly, and dropped to the bottom of the cage where he sat quivering in total shock.

The horrified look on Audrey's face spoke volumes of fear as she turned with tearful eyes, clutching the cage against her body. She walked quickly toward the quietness of the library.

"Chip, you get right back here and sit," Benjamin ordered.

"Get that dog on a leash, young man or he's out on his ear," Miss Reed directed with a glare, as she hurried to reassure Audrey.

"What am I gonna do?" Benjamin directed his stressful plea at me.

"Don't you have a leash?" Edgar Granlund said.

"No. I guess Chip will have to go outside," Benjamin said with a sad face.

"Hey, I've got an extra corn string tie in the bottom of my gunny sack," said Edgar. "You can use that. It'll work okay if you hang on to it really tight. Want to try it? You'll have to hold it tight, though. And I need it back when we're done so I can sack up my turtles."

"Hey, thanks." Benjamin tied the corn string loosely around Chip's neck and the patient dog obeyed his command to 'sit' once again.

"Where did ya get that fancy rope?" Sid Jones snickered at Benjamin's makeshift leash. Sid placed a covered cardboard box on the table and ran his dirty hand through his brown matted hair. He kicked the air in front of Chip's face, as he walked past Benjamin's desk, his sarcastic smile showing his chipped tooth. A low throated growl emerged from Chip's throat.

"My leash will work fine," Benjamin answered. "And, don't tease my dog."

By now, most of our class had become wise to Sid's taunts, and no one was falling for the irritating arguments he wanted to start. I noticed that Sid's box did not have a note card of information on it. I wondered what was in the box, but he looked at me with a sneer, so I didn't ask.

Miss Reed rang the bell. She held her head high and stretched to her full five feet tall.

"Children and visitors, our class will come to order," she instructed.

I noticed a hint of a smile wash over her face as she specifically gazed at the 'visitors.' They included several parents, grandparents, and creatures that students had brought in cages, buckets, boxes, gunny sacks, and bowls for the honor of appearing in the Apple Valley School Pet Display.

"The pet exhibit will be first on our plan of the day," she continued. "The animals you have brought with you may become restless and parents may want to transport them home after our viewing.

"Students, stand next to your pet's cage or container. Other students and visitors may have questions. Your card explaining what you have learned from being a pet owner should be on your cage or container. If your pet is not in a cage, you may explain this information to those admiring your animal."

Audrey Swingley looked calm again, as she placed her bird cage on the table between Amy Hall's goldfish bowl and a box containing a hermit crab aquarium. Students and visitors checked out each pet exhibit holding some of the creatures, and observing the others.

"These are my turtles, 'U. R. Slowsky' and 'I. M. Speedo'," Edgar Granlund said as I walked up to his display. "I enjoy racing these guys… 'I. M. Speedo' usually wins."

"That sounds fun…we should have had them race today," I said.

The note of information on Edgar's box stated: "My turtles are painted turtles. I enjoy watching them race each other. Slowsky is the largest and slowest. Speedo, the smallest, usually wins the race! I caught them in the pond and have kept them in a stock tank for a few weeks. It has been fun to have them for pets, but I will release them back into the pond on our farm before cold weather comes and winter freeze-up."

Sid's box sat next to Edgar's turtles.

"What's in your box, Sid?" I asked as I moved along the display table.

"I'll open the cover for a quick peek," he answered. With mischief glowing in his eyes, he slowly raised the lid and watched the action with a grin. A striped garter snake rose up searching the corner of the box for the nearest exit. Sid did nothing to stop the snake's escape. With one more slither his 'pet' squirmed his way out of the box and onto the table, then to the floor, his forked tongue waving wildly.

Sid's hard laugh was louder than the screaming girls. Now everyone cleared away from the display table and watched with panic.

The snake wove its way around the table legs, as students and visitors stepped aside. Sid's wiry friend slipped between the rows of desks, setting off more shrieks of fear from the young girls sitting near the front of the room. Determined to find its get away, the snake wriggled toward the back of the room. But Miss Reed was about to end the chase. He was trapped in a corner. Our teacher's swift hand grabbed the poor reptile by the back of his head.

"Sidney Jones," she said. "Bring your box over here and take this creature outside. Then you will not be tempted to set it free inside our schoolroom again."

Sid's sarcastic smile returned as he picked up the snake by the tail, swung it around a few times to taunt the frightened first graders, threw it in the box, and then carried it outdoors.

As our visitors shook their heads and student's conversation resumed, I walked over to Jesse's rabbit cages to check on her display.

"How's it going, Jesse?" I asked.

"Great," she said. "What a morning! I'm glad that snake didn't come over here. I hate snakes. I'm glad Miss Reed made Sid take him out of here. I'll bet he let him go on purpose."

"Yeah, he sure did," I said. "I had no idea what was in his box. When Sid lifted the cover, I should have grabbed the snake right away. But I guess it would've spoiled all his fun!"

"I'm having a great time talking about my rabbits and showing them to everyone," Jessie said. "I'm going to have some baby bunnies for sale soon. I want them to go to good homes. Do you know anyone that wants a rabbit for a pet?"

"I can't think of anyone right now. Don't sell one to Sid. He'd probably treat it mean," I said.

"No way. I wouldn't sell any rabbits to him," Jessie agreed.

The card of information on Jesse's cages said: *I've learned responsibility through caring for my 'Holland Lop-Eared' rabbits. They make good pets and are easy to raise. I meet many interesting people who come to buy rabbits from our farm, and I also raise my rabbits for my 4-H projects.*

"Want to hold one of my rabbits, Eddie?" Jessie asked.

"Sure, let me hold 'Pokey.'" I said. "Do you sell some of your rabbits to pet stores?"

"Sometimes we do. But people in the county know that I raise rabbits. So most of our sales are directly to people who come to our farm and buy them."

Pokey sat contentedly, as I fed him a carrot. I figured maybe

Benjamin and his younger brothers might enjoy a pet like this. I looked around the classroom for Benjamin and Chip, but they were no where in sight.

Chapter Thirty-Three

I put Pokey back in his cage and walked over to look out the classroom window that overlooked the playground. I saw Benjamin standing at the edge of the woods. He held the corn string rope, but Chip was not beside him.

"Miss Reed, may I go and see if Benjamin needs help?" I asked. "It seems his dog is missing."

"You may check, but we cannot take time from our school lessons to hunt for lost dogs. That pet did not have a proper leash in the first place, you know."

"Yes Ma'am." I said as I hurried outside, only to find Benjamin in tears.

"He ran off, Eddie. I took him out here to go potty, but then Sid came outside. He lifted his snake up in the air and called Chip over to see it. I tried to hold onto him, but Chip burst after the snake, and the corn string broke. Then Sid threw the snake right out in front of him. Chip went crazy. He chased the snake as it slithered out behind those rocks. Chip followed it, and he barked and growled, and then he disappeared further into the woods.

"I've been calling him over and over, but he won't come back. What should I do? He'll get lost back there," Benjamin cried.

"Miss Reed says you have to come back inside the school," I said. "Maybe Chip will find his own way home, or he might be waiting outside for us when school is over. You have to quit crying now."

We walked into the school as Benjamin tried to dry his eyes on the sleeve of his jacket. Parents and grandparents were leaving, with a few of the pets. Other students would wait until after school for their parents to pick up their animals.

"Hey, cry-baby, where'd your stupid dog run off to," Sid asked Benjamin in crude sarcasm.

"I don't know," Benjamin answered with a sober face. "You don't care anyway, so why ask?"

"Here Edgar, thanks for letting me borrow this. I'm sorry it broke," Benjamin said as he handed the left over piece of corn string to Edgar.

"I guess it wasn't strong enough after all," Edgar said.

"It would have worked fine if Chip wouldn't have chased after Sid's snake," Benjamin said. "Chip jerked so hard. Sid always has to start trouble."

"Hey, look at little cry-baby Wagner trying to stick the blame on me," Sid came up behind the boys, trying to keep the argument going. The boy's voices rose loud enough for Miss Reed to hear.

"Sidney Jones, we've had enough of your tomfoolery for today. Come up to the blackboard. I have some extra math problems for you to do. That should keep your mind busy for the next hour. You've had entirely too much time to create mischief."

Sid strolled up to the front of the classroom with his usual obnoxious smirk. He took precise aim to fire a hard rolled spitball at Benjamin on his way to the front of the room.

"The first-graders will receive their new Dick and Jane books today," Miss Reed said. "We will look at the first story together. The other grades may go to the library and choose books for the Raceway Reading Contest. You may choose up to three books each week."

On my way to the library, I watched Benjamin. The spitball had hit him right in his left eye. He rubbed his eye and glared at Sid, but there was little else he could do. Sid was a bully, and the best thing Benjamin could do right now was to stay out of his way. How could a little kid defend himself against a kid the size of big Sid Jones?

Benjamin covered his sore eye, and tried to look interested in his first Dick and Jane reading book. A few weeks ago, Miss Reed sent home flash cards of words that he practiced with his mother. Now he would see those words in his reading book.

The Apple River School Library received many new books for our school year. I chose *Island Stallion* by Walter Farley. Since there were so many chores for me at the Wagner's, I checked out only one book. I hoped I could get this one read before the due date.

"Students, after you have chosen your library books, enter your name on the Raceway Contest Bulletin Board. You will each receive a paper race car. You may move your car one space along the raceway track for each book you read.

"After reading your book, I'm asking you to write a book report on the book using these forms on my desk. This allows me to know that you are reading and understanding each book you choose.

"The Raceway Contest prize given to the reader of the most books is a set of deluxe art pencils and a sketch tablet. You may view them in the glass case in the library."

* * *

At the end of the school day, parents came to pick up the children with pets and soon the schoolroom was empty.

"Thanks for helping me water my rabbits, today," Jessie said as she wheeled her chair toward their car. "You saved me a lot of trips."

"Hey, I like your rabbits," I said. "Your dad built great cages. I'm glad you brought your rabbit project in to show our class. See you tomorrow."

We boys were the last to leave the schoolyard. We saw no sign of Chip anywhere.

"I walked through the edge of the woods behind the school one more time," Benjamin said. "But he isn't back there."

"I don't think you should worry," Daniel said. "I'll bet he just followed his nose and trotted back home. Dogs can do that. He probably found a shortcut."

"Yep, they have a real good sense of direction," I added. "The farm is just up the road. He's probably at home waiting for us."

"I hope you're right," Benjamin said. "But I wish I would never have thought about bringing Chip to any old pet day at school. Chip should have stayed home on the farm where he belongs."

I saw tears start up in his eyes again. His left eye looked mighty red and sore. If Sid continued to pick on Benjamin, the rest of us from the Wagner house would have to set him straight.

Chapter Thirty-Four

We walked up the Wagner's driveway hoping to see Chip bound toward us with his usual greeting. However, no dog appeared.

"If we ever take Chip off the farm again, we will find a leash," I said. "We shouldn't have taken him to school without one."

As we walked into the house, Benjamin raced into the living room where his mom rested on the sofa.

"Hi kids, how was your day…and how did Chip like school?"

Benjamin's sad face enhanced the story as he told his mother about the unhappy experience, and spiteful Sid with his snake that caused the trouble.

"I couldn't hold Chip back from running after that slithery thing, and I wanted to keep looking for him in the woods, but they made me go back into school," Benjamin said with tears starting to spill out of his blue eyes. "I never should have taken Chip away from home in the first place."

"Maybe Chip will still find his way home," Janet Wagner said. "Let's not give up hope yet." She reached over and gave Benjamin a hug then she noticed his very red left eye.

"Benjamin, what's wrong with your eye?"

"It got bumped at school," he said.

He rubbed the tears from his eyes and walked out the back door.

"We'd better get our clothes changed and get the cows up to the barn," I said to the older boys. "We'll keep a look out for Chip. I think he'll find his way back home."

* * *

Cold weather hit hard. On an early morning in late November, Mr. Wagner came into the barn where I was feeding the calves.

"This dang car is ready for the junk heap! There's no money to buy a new one. The cold weather keeps the engine from firing," he said. "I've tried at least ten times and it won't start. I'm gonna hitch up the team and I want you drive them so they will pull the car to get it going. It'll pop the clutch and I'll be off. I'm nearly late for work now, so hurry up! Come and help me."

I pulled on my barn gloves that were full of holes. I needed new ones and Mrs. Wagner had promised I would get them on the next shopping trip. Somehow, that never happened. I overheard Mr. Wagner complain about no money every time he went to town, and he never brought home work gloves for me or any of his boys.

"You gotta hang on to the reins of this team 'cause the horses are feisty when it's cold," Mr. Wagner said.

The horses strained hard against the weight of the auto. Then… "sput sput, sput—vroom." The auto started. Mr. Wagner jumped out of his car, believing I had the team under control as he unhitched them from the car.

"I can't hold 'em," I yelled as they charged ahead. My hands were numb with cold and there was no way I could hold the reins tight enough to control this team that now wanted to run in the brisk wintry morning air.

Fortunately for me, the horses made a circle of the farmyard and trotted back to the barn.

"You stupid kid!" Mr. Wagner yelled at me. "I told you to hang onto the reins. Can't you do anything right? Now I'll be late for work because you didn't follow my orders."

Donald Wagner couldn't control his rage or think through the situation. Anger flooded his face. He grabbed the reins of the horse harness.

"You stand right there," he ordered. "You'll learn to do what I tell you to do, and do it right the first time." He beat me on my back and legs and yelled, "Now get out of my sight."

John and Daniel heard their father yelling and came out of the barn. They watched with sober faces at their father's angry outburst and walked with me back into the barn as Mr. Wagner drove off to work.

I determined not to cry when Mr. Wagner beat me. But inside, my feelings reflected a broken mirror…shattered emotions of fear, pain, and rage swirled together.

I'm sick of working on someone else's farm and being blamed for things I can't control, I thought. What good does it do to try my best? What reward is there in that? When something bad happens… I get blamed as though it was my fault.

After Mr. Wagner left for work, we boys unhitched and fed the team. I didn't feel much like breakfast, but we needed to eat and get ready for school.

As we sat by the breakfast table, a black pick-up drove in the driveway. There was a knock at the door. Benjamin ran to answer.

"Hello," he said to the stranger.

"Hi there, I'm Joe Flannery. You folks missing a dog?" the older man asked, as he pointed to a dog in the passenger seat of his truck.

"Yes, we are," Benjamin answered.

"A dog got caught in my trap line in the woods way back behind Apple Valley School."

Benjamin ran out to the truck. By now the rest of us left our breakfast and followed him.

"That's Chip," Benjamin said excitedly.

"I thought I'd seen a dog about that size and color when I've gone past your place. His foot got hurt, but it's healed up pretty good. Can't figure out what he was doing way back there…"

Mr. Flannery opened the truck door, and Chip jumped out.

"You're home, Boy. I'm so glad you came back to us," Benjamin said, as he hugged his dog.

"It's his left front paw that was caught. I wrapped it in a rag with some ointment for a while, so it would heal. He still favors it some. I know he's your dog for sure…look at him wag his tail and lick the boy's face," Mr. Flannery said to me. "Well, guess I'd best be getting on now. Glad to have found the dog's rightful owner."

"Thank you Mr. Flannery," I said.

"We're glad to have him home," Benjamin said with a huge grin. "Thank you, sir."

Chip's tail wagged determinedly as Benjamin gave him another big hug.

Chapter Thirty-Five

"Eddie, please come up to my desk before you go out for recess," Miss Reed said.

The schoolroom emptied as the children pulled on their jackets, boots, hats, and mittens, to play outside on this cold snowy day. What did I do now? I thought.

"I have to ask a question that has been troubling me for several weeks," Miss Reed said. "How much free time to you have as a foster child in the Wagner home?"

I didn't like being put on the spot. But I hated skirting the truth a whole lot more. I decided to answer the question exactly as my daily routine allowed.

"I help with chores and milking before I come to school. I do chores and clean the barn after school. I help get supper on the table because Mrs. Wagner is on bed rest. She's going to have a baby. After supper, we milk the cows. When I get done helping with milking, I need to get into the house and help the little ones get ready for bed. Mrs. Wagner needs me to do that, too, because she can't be on her feet, going up and down the stairs. Some of the older kids try to help me with dishes, and we clean up the kitchen. We have a neighbor who brings in casseroles and other food to help out."

"When do you have time to study and read, Eddie?" Miss Reed asked with a look of deep concern.

"Actually, there isn't much time left after my chores. I open my books and my eyes close, and the next thing, I fall asleep with my clothes on."

"Is that why you returned your library book without completing a book report?" Miss Reed asked.

"Yes. I like to read, but I don't have extra time for library books when I'm trying to read the lesson books I brought home."

"That's not right. Don't your foster parents know you should be allowed time to do your schoolwork?"

"Well, right now it seems that they're just trying to keep things going at that house. Mrs. Wagner would do more, but she has to rest all the time or she might lose her baby. Mr. Wagner has to keep working on his day job to pay the bills. It's a struggle for everybody, I guess."

"That might be, but their problems certainly are not yours. You are doing the work of a farm hand, and a baby sitter, and you're a young boy. Why you're not much older than Daniel, their oldest son."

"I have to do what I'm told or Mr. Wagner makes it mean," I said.

"Eddie, you're my student and I know you can do much better in class than you're doing. I'm certain it is because you don't have time to give to your studies. I have no choice but to report this to the welfare board. You are not to be overworked as a farm hand with no time to do your schoolwork."

"Miss Reed, I'd appreciate if you didn't say I complained," I said with pangs of worry going through my mind. "If Mr. Wagner thinks I came to you to belly ache about how I've been treated, he'll really lay it on me."

"No one is going to know about our talk. Your dropping grades speak for themselves. I know you can do much better than you are doing now, if you have time to study."

I nodded. I went to the cloakroom and grabbed my jacket, and pulled on my four-buckle overshoes. I was putting on my gloves when Miss Reed walked by me on her way to the library.

"Eddie, are those the only gloves you have to wear?" Miss Reed asked as she noticed my gloves full of holes.

"Yes, ma'am."

"That's ridiculous! I can't tell parents how to dress their children, but you are a welfare child...a ward of St. Croix County. That means, Eddie, that you should at least have adequate clothing to keep you warm. Your foster parents should be able to purchase you a pair of gloves to keep out the cold."

She sighed and shook her head.

"May I go outside now, Miss Reed?"

"Yes, Eddie, go ahead."

* * *

"Hey kids, that's Gertie Lou's car by the house," John said, as we walked up the driveway on our way home from school. "I wonder what she's doing here at this time of the day."

"We'll soon find out, won't we," I said.

"Hey, what did Miss Reed want to talk to you about, today Eddie?" Daniel asked.

"She just said I had to study harder 'cause my grades were falling behind."

"I hate schoolwork. I'd rather work on the farm all the time. If I was older, I bet my dad would let me quit school and work for him on the farm. I could get a lot done around here if I didn't go to school."

"That wouldn't be too smart, Daniel. If you're going to run a farming operation on your own, you need to have mathematics and science, and be a good reader, too," I said.

"Why couldn't I just feed and milk the cows, and keep the barn clean, and take care of the calves? I know how to do that."

"Yes, but do you know how to buy and sell cows and calves, and decide how much money you can afford for feed, and…"

"Hey," Daniel interrupted. "I can learn what I need to know about farming from my dad. I don't need to stay in school and listen to any old teacher tell me what she thinks is important."

"I think you'd be a better farmer if you graduated from high school, Daniel," I said.

As usual, Benjamin was first to rush into the house. He wanted to be the first to tell his mother about his school day.

"Hi kids," Gertie Lou greeted us.

"Where's Mom?" Benjamin asked.

"You're dad came home to take her to the hospital because she's not feeling well. I came to stay with the little kids."

"When did they leave?" Daniel asked.

"It was almost noon. Maybe you'll have a brother or sister before the day is over."

"Really?" Benjamin said in a surprised tone.

"Well, you never can tell for sure…it could happen that way," Gertie Lou said with a warm smile.

"Let's go out and get the chores started," I said. "If your dad is at the hospital, we may be milking the cows alone tonight."

Chapter Thirty-Six

"Eddie... Eddie... Get up. I've got to talk to you," Mr. Wagner's loud, demanding voice called.

I rubbed the sleep from my eyes and pulled on my pants and a shirt, and then hurried downstairs.

"What's wrong?" I asked my foster father who looked unusually grim.

"Mrs. Wagner's had the baby. It's a girl. I'm afraid we're facing another high-cost hospital bill, so I'm selling off four milk cows. That will leave only six to milk through the winter. Then we'll have some money to pay the hospital and doctor.

"Get your jacket on and come to the barn to help me move these cows into a different pen. I sold them to a farmer who will pick them up when you kids are at school today."

I glanced at the clock and noticed it read 12:30a.m. What was this man thinking of? In five hours we'd be up to do the chores and milking? Couldn't we do this cattle moving then?

I grabbed my jacket, pulled on my boots, and followed Mr. Wagner out to the barn. The night air sent a chill that crept through my jacket and pant legs. I hadn't taken time to put on long underwear or even grab my gloves, such as they were.

When we entered the barn, Mr. Wagner flipped on the light switch. The dim light cast an eerie look over his animals. They appeared unconcerned to see us at this time of night, until we got inside the pen and began trying to move them.

"Hold this gate open while I get the right cows directed in," he ordered. "Be sure you don't let any of them get around you."

My boots squished down into the stinking manure that oozed on the floor of the pen in which the cows stood. I thought of Mr. Fletcher's clean barn where I had worked for such a short time. How different these farmers valued the care of their livestock.

Mr. Wagner circled behind Clara, one of their oldest cows, and prodded her ahead into the pen he had prepared.

"Watch it now," he warned. Don't let her push her way out when I get the others."

My boots continued to suck down into the muck, but I hung onto the gate and watched Clara as she snorted and puffed, steam rising from her nostrils. Then he edged Dolly in to follow. As she entered the pen with Clara, her big eyes looked wide with astonishment. Sally, too, and last of all, old Katie. All these were singled out from the others and put into this holding pen. These cows would be sold. I knew that old Katie, as well as Sally, had not been producing much milk in the last month. They would not be a great loss to the family's milk supply.

"Now you'd better get back to bed so you can get up to milk the cows. Be sure you milk these four cows, too, before we send them away. Get Daniel and John to help you milk and do the other chores before school. I'm leaving early to make up some of the time I missed at my work yesterday when I was at the hospital."

* * *

The calendar said it was the day before Thanksgiving. That meant four days off from school and a traditional meal to celebrate the reason to give thanks. We had been studying about the first Thanksgiving in school. We even performed a short play and gave several readings about this day that celebrated the way the pilgrims and their new found neighbors did a long time ago.

I thought about my own reasons for being thankful. I was glad that I had a visit with Ellie. However, being separated from her and never knowing if she was okay was sad. And then, what about my other siblings? I continued to think about them. Who were they? Did they live in Wisconsin, too? I was determined that some day I would find them. It might take a long time, but I would hunt until I found the clues that could open the doors to the rest of the family secret.

"Hey kids," Gertie Lou said. "You might want to see who's driving up the driveway."

All the older Wagner children and I looked out the windows to see Mr. Wagner's car drive up through the light snow on this late November afternoon.

"Mom's here with our new baby," shouted Benjamin.

"Our baby?" Nathan said and clapped his hands.

My smiling foster mom walked through the door with her new little bundle of life.

With snowflakes melting on her hat and coat, she greeted her waiting children.

"Come and meet your new sister, Julia," she said as she sat down in the living room rocker. "Who do you think she looks like?"

"She has blond hair like the twins," John said.

"Her eyes are shut so we can't see them," Benjamin said.

"Well, I've seen them and they are dark blue," their mom said.

"Where's Dad?" Daniel asked.

"He's getting some things from the car," Janet Wagner said. "You do know what day it is tomorrow, don't you?"

"Yes, Thanksgiving," John said.

"You'll have a Thanksgiving dinner with us, won't you, Gertie Lou?" Janet asked.

"Sure, I will," Gertie Lou said with a grin.

"I asked Donald to stop and buy a few extra things for our dinner, so it will feel like a holiday meal. I know he doesn't think we can afford it, but a touch here and there will be good for us all.

"He bought a small turkey. We have our own potatoes and other garden vegetables. I asked him to buy some cranberries and a box of brown sugar and…oh yes, coffee, we're almost out of that. We have apples stored in the cellar to make a pie. It all sounded so good when I was planning it, but now I feel so tired. I think I have to go and lie down before the baby wakes up and needs to nurse again."

"Guess what, Janet… I decided apple pie sounded good for a Thanksgiving meal for your family, so I already made one this afternoon."

"You're a great friend…what would we do without you?"

"Go lie down now, before the baby starts crying. And Janet, when you feel up to it, there's a number here for either you or Donald to call. He called several days ago. I put it by the telephone. I believe it is Eddie's social worker at St. Croix County Welfare Office. He said either one of you should call him as soon as you returned home, but it's late now. I don't think you need to do anything about it until after Thanksgiving. I told him that you were in the hospital."

"Okay, I'll do it after the holiday, then. Thanks Gertie Lou."

"Gertie Lou," I said cautiously, "What was that all about… I mean about the social worker and the phone number?"

"Oh, I don't think it's anything for you to worry about, Eddie," Gertie Lou tried to assure me. However, I wasn't feeling reassured. No one knew about the conversation I had with Miss Reed. I believed that her concern over the fact that I had too much work to do and no time to study might have something to do with this phone call. Now the same old questions began to loom up into my mind. Would I be on the move again? Would it be soon? Where would I go? Would it be better or worse than where I am now?

Chapter Thirty-Seven

Thanksgiving Day arrived with snowy wind gusts blowing up a ferocious chill. We were forced to pull our caps and scarves tightly around our faces when we went outside.

"I'll carry these pitchers of milk to the house," I told the boys when we were done milking. "Finish feeding the calves and we'll see what we can do to help your mom."

Gertie Lou's truck drove up the driveway as we came out of the barn. She took several bags and a box out of her pick-up and walked with us into the house.

"Hi, kids, Happy Thanksgiving!" she said. "Do you want to set these bags and this box on the table for me, please?"

"Happy Thanksgiving!" we said in chorus, as we helped her with the containers.

"How's that new baby sister?" Gertie Lou asked as she took off her coat and hat and walked into the living room where the bassinet stood. "She's sleeping as soundly as ever. Has anyone seen her eyes yet?"

"I haven't," Ben said. "She even keeps 'em shut when she cries."

"Hey, that turkey sure smells good," Gertie Lou said, as she walked back into the kitchen and hung her wraps on the coat rack.

"Yeah, my mom told my dad what to do, and he put the turkey in the oven," John said. "Mom's resting right now. Dad went on an errand."

"That's good. She need's lots of rest. It's hard work having a baby."

"Hi there! I thought I heard voices out here," Janet Wagner said, as she walked into the kitchen. "Baby Julia is going to wake up soon. See her stirring over there, kids?"

Within minutes the stirring turned into a squeaky cry, and then it was time for a diaper change. With all the brothers and sisters for an audience, Janet Wagner changed Julia's tiny diaper.

"Can we call her 'Julie' instead of 'Julia'... I think it sounds better," Benjamin said.

"I guess that can be her nickname if you wish," Mrs. Wagner said. "I rather like it myself. It seems more—little girl-like."

So from then on the smallest Wagner child became Julie.

Mrs. Wagner proceeded to wrap Julie warmly in a soft receiving blanket, and then she sat down in the rocker to nurse her.

I had never seen a human mother nurse her child before this moment. It made me feel awkward. However, the Wagner children did not seem to notice or care about watching Julie nurse. It seemed to be routine for them. That's what their mom did to nourish their baby sister.

"Kids, why don't you join me in the kitchen and we'll set the table for our Thanksgiving meal?" Gertie Lou asked.

"What's in this box and these bags?" John asked

"I brought some mixed nuts for snacking, and some chocolate chip cookies, and in the box are some ribbon candy curls, and one more pie...a pecan one," Gertie Lou said. "In that brown bag are special Thanksgiving napkins. We can put one on each plate."

"So, do we need twelve plates then?" John asked. I saw Gertie Lou look over at my foster mom with a smile.

"Put on one extra plate, John," Gertie Lou answered, continuing her mischievous grin. "Just to make sure we have enough."

I counted out the silverware and set them on the table. Then I took down glasses from the cupboard for each place setting.

"Eddie, will you skim off some of that thick cream from the top of one of the pitchers of milk, please?" Gertie Lou asked, as she handed me a bowl. "I'm going to whip it up to top off our pies."

"Sure I will…that sound's great," I answered. I was careful to skim off the richest portion of the cream that had risen to the top of the pitcher. Mrs. Wagner had told me that only the rich cream whipped up into good peaks for the topping used for desserts.

The potatoes were cooking and the veggies were nearly done. This meal was shaping up to be a winner, but I wondered where Mr. Wagner had gone. I noticed the smile and looks that my foster mom and Gertie Lou gave each other. Was there some kind of a surprise that no one else knew about?

Soon the Wagner car pulled up into the driveway. I looked out the window, but I was shocked at what I saw. I didn't say a word. In fact, I was speechless. Who in the world decided to invite the family's most disgruntled relative? And why on this holiday when everyone wanted to be joyful, happy, and thankful?

"I heard the car, I think Dad's here," Daniel said as he came over to the window and stood by me to have a look. "Oh, no Mom…why? Why her?"

"Who is it Daniel?" Who's here?" John asked as he joined us at the window.

"Oh, Mom…" John groaned.

I stood in silence with solemn thoughts of my last meeting with our guest.

"Now kids, it's Thanksgiving. It's a day when we can show our love for each other. We have to be kind to her. She's all alone in the world," Janet Wagner's voice faded softly away as the door opened.

"Happy Thanksgiving to ya," Aunt Bertha said as she looked us over with a bit less of a scowl than usual.

"Happy Thanksgiving, Bertha," Janet Wagner said, as she looked toward her husband's older sister with a soft smile. She laid Julia in her bassinette and walked over to Aunt Bertha and gave her a polite hug.

"Come right in," Janet said. "Let me take your coat and scarf. I'll hang them up."

"I brought ya some pickled herring; not sure if ya all like it, but it's family holiday tradition with us Wagner's. Donald tells me ya popped another one out of the hatch. A girl this time, was it?"

"Yes, Bertha, a beautiful little daughter, named Julia. Benjamin has decided her nickname should be Julie."

"Never liked nick-names. Don't seem to be right callin' ya somethin' other than your own name," Bertha stated pushing her glasses further up on her nose.

Benjamin looked over at me and shook his head. I winked at him and grinned as Aunt Bertha continued.

"Is that the little thing over in the crib?"

"Yes, that's our little Julie. Come get a closer look…would you like to hold her?"

"Mercy me, no! She'd near break apart on me. You're sure she's okay being that small and all?"

"Oh yes, she is strong and healthy. Just like our other eight blessings."

"Blessings—that's what ya call em, blessings, huh?"

"I think it's time for you all to find a place to sit down at the table now," Gertie Lou said. "Our food is ready. Donald, you did a great job with this turkey and stuffing."

"Bertha, you sit right there alongside Donald," Mrs. Wagner said. "And the rest of you kids know where your places are. I'll sit here by the twins and help them fill their plates."

I could see Mr. Wagner looked a bit uncomfortable as his sister took the chair beside his. He moved over as far as he could toward Daniel to give her plenty of room.

Inviting crabby Aunt Bertha was certainly an amazing surprise that I wasn't prepared for. By the looks on the other kid's faces, it seemed they were as shocked as I was.

"Okay, before we eat, we are going to say a table prayer," Janet Wagner said. "This is Thanksgiving Day. We have much to thank God for. Many things have happened this summer to make me think about my life. When I was young, I used to pray. Then my parents died and I thought God forgot about me. When Eddie came to live with us, he reminded me that God does answer prayer. He told me the story of how his sister got lost in a snowstorm. He said God helped him find her. He encouraged me to pray again.

"I've been thinking about that. When I've been pregnant with Julie, we nearly lost her. I've been praying that God would keep her safe inside me, and let her be born alive. God answered my prayer, and I want to thank Him for that today. I want to thank Him for all of my children, for my husband, and Gertie Lou our dear friend, and Aunt Bertha, and Eddie.

"Dear Lord,

Thank you for this wonderful food; for our family, our friends, our farm, and most of all your love and protection over us. Thank you that what Eddie says is true: *You God are with us wherever we go, and you hear our prayers. Amen.*"

"Thank you Janet," Gertie Lou said with tears in her eyes. "Let's bring the food to the table."

Chapter Thirty-Eight

"Ya did a good job, Donald," Aunt Bertha said. "This turkey's tasty."

That was the first compliment I ever heard Bertha give her brother. In fact, hearing something kind come out of her mouth was amazing.

"I'll have some more of that squash, if ya don't mind," she continued, as she pushed her glasses up on her nose. "I 'spose you grew this in your garden."

"Yes, Bertha," Janet Wagner said. "All the vegetables were grown in our garden. Would someone please pass me the pickled herring that Aunt Bertha brought?"

"Do you like that stuff, Mom?" Benjamin asked

"I'm going to eat a piece because it's Thanksgiving," his mother said with a grin. "Do you want to try some?"

"No thanks," Benjamin wrinkled up his nose.

"How about some herring for you, Gertie Lou?" Janet asked.

"I believe I'll pass," she said with a smile.

"I'll take some down here at this end of the table," Donald Wagner said. "I haven't had herring for years, Bertha. It is a treat to me."

Bertha made no comment, but with a grin, she took the herring jar and pushed her potatoes over on her plate to make a small space for another piece of the pickled fish she loved.

"Ya know Mama wouldn't serve Thanksgiving dinner without pickled herring, Donald," she said. "That's why I knew ya would be enjoying it as much as I always do."

I could see John squirm in his chair and make a sour face at Daniel as their father passed the jar toward them. I figured they would leave the rest of the pieces in the jar for their father and Aunt Bertha. It was all I could do not to plug my nose when I got a whiff of the stinky fish.

"Ya probably wonder why I fuss about you so, Donald. After our parents died, I felt so responsible for your well-being," Aunt Bertha said. "Ya were such a young lad and so foolish.

"I was old enough to take care of ya. Mama and Papa left us the house and enough money for both of us to get by, but ya always did things your own way. Ya wouldn't hear of getting a job and staying in the house with me. Ya ran off and married Janet and then started having all these kids. Look how ya live on this run-down farm…and I sit in that big lonely house by myself. What would Mama think of that? Can't ya see why I gave up and got so angry with ya?"

I could see tears in Janet Wagner's eyes. She put her head down and sat quietly at her end of the table. Silence fell over the meal. No one offered any response to Aunt Bertha's crude remarks.

Donald Wagner got up from the table and walked over to the kitchen cupboard.

"Are we going to eat these pies or are they just for looks?" he asked, ignoring his sister's irritating question.

"We're certainly going to eat them," Gertie Lou said with a grin. "And right now would be a great time to dish them up."

Aunt Bertha shook her head and her face took on a disgusted look. She ended her comment on the Wagner past history.

"What kind of pie would you like, Aunt Bertha? We have apple or pecan or a slice of each," Gertie Lou offered. "And fresh whipped cream on top, if you like."

"I'd like apple pie, like my mama would have made," she said. "I don't need whipped cream. She never served it like that," she responded in a grumpy voice.

I noticed a big grin on Gertie Lou's face as she continued taking the pie orders.

"And Donald, what kind of pie can I cut for you?"

"Make mine pecan, please, with plenty of whipped cream."

"Why Donald," Aunt Bertha said with raised eyebrows, you always wanted Mama's apple pie. What's going on? Has everything about you changed?"

"It's good to try new things, Bertha. That's your problem. You always want to live in the past. You can't always do everything in life the same old way," Mr. Wagner told his sister.

She shook her head and exclaimed, "Not all change is good, Donald. Remember I told you that. We had a good Mama and she did the best she could trying to raise us alone after Papa died."

When everyone finished dessert, it was time for us to help clear the dishes. We kids hurried outside in the falling snow that had begun to pile-up at a rapid pace.

"Look, Eddie, catch these snowflakes on your tongue," Benjamin said. "See, it's just like another dessert."

"I'm too full to eat another dessert, Benjamin," I said. "But let's try this, guys. Everyone line up in a straight line and fall back in the snow. Now move your arms and legs back and forth and then get up. See, now we have a row of snow angels."

"I think we should build a snow fort," John said. "The snow is sticking really great. We can roll large snowballs and pack them together to build the walls."

"Okay," Daniel said.

"I'll help," Benjamin said as he joined his brothers.

As we began rolling snow balls, Aunt Bertha and Mr. Wagner came out the back door and walked toward the car.

"Eddie, the snow is starting to come down thick and heavy," Mr. Wagner said. "I've got to get Aunt Bertha to the bus stop before our road gets a lot worse. I'm depending on you and the boys to get the chores started and the milking done."

"Okay," I said.

As they drove out the driveway, I thought about what an odd relationship Mr. Wagner and his sister Bertha had. I wished I could see my sister Ellie. We were close. These two acted like it was an effort to be together. I wished Ellie and I had spent Thanksgiving together.

"Daniel, I'm going in the house to check what time it is," I said. "If we have to milk the cows alone tonight, I don't want to start late. We need to be done before your dad gets back."

As I stepped in the door, I heard Mrs. Wagner on the telephone.

"You mean you're coming to pick him up tomorrow?"

I stood quietly in the kitchen doorway and listened.

"Well of course I would have called you right away, but I was in the hospital. I just gave birth to a baby and got home yesterday. And today is Thanksgiving. My goodness, what can be the rush? What do you mean, he's overworked? His grades are that low? I didn't realize he needed to have more time to study. Well yes, he does do a lot of work around here. Yes, he does the milking, and the calve chores. He has helped me inside because I was on bed rest, but that was before I had our new baby. We have nine children now with the new baby. Yes, with Eddie there are ten children.

"You've already made you're decision? Can't we discuss it? All right, I'll tell him. Nine o'clock tomorrow morning. Okay. I'm so surprised. I had no idea. I wish someone would have said something sooner. Yes, I will. Goodbye."

Janet Wagner turned and saw me standing in her kitchen, my wet boots dripping on her kitchen rug. Her eyes filled with tears as she looked at me and said:

"Eddie, did you hear? The welfare is moving you."

Chapter Thirty-Nine

I woke up with a start. It was light outside. Mr. Wagner hadn't called me to milk the cows. What was going on?

I checked the big boy's beds. They must have gotten up, but I hadn't heard a thing. I pulled on my clothes and ran downstairs.

"Eddie, you're not doing the chores this morning. Mr. Wagner and the big boys milked the cows before he went to work. Get ready for the day, and then pack up your box. I'm fixing a good breakfast. Your social worker will be here in a couple of hours."

"Okay," I said and I headed out to the outhouse. My good friend Chip ran to me when I stepped out the door, his tail wagging a friendly greeting.

"C'mon Boy, wanna race?" I challenged him. I knew I would miss this dog most. He was a good buddy.

As I came back into the house, I went upstairs to pack up my things, Benjamin followed me close behind me.

"Hey, Eddie, Mom says you're leaving our house," he said. He looked at me with sad eyes and continued. "How come they're taking you away?"

"Welfare kids live in a lot of different places, Benjamin. Today, it's moving day again," I said

I put my flashlight with its dead batteries, my baseball and glove, and Half-Pint's ribbon, safely in the bottom of the box. On top of these things I laid my clothes. I placed my Bible Story Book on top to hold every thing else down tight. My green glass keeper and my watch fob from the curious stranger were safe in my pants pocket.

"Will we ever see you again?" Benjamin asked.

"I don't know, but look at this," I said, as I picked up the metal red horse that the Mobil Oil station attendant had given me. "I'm giving this to you, so you'll have something to remember me by."

"Thanks, Eddie!"

I felt a grin spill over my face as I looked at this little kid who seemed so pleased to receive this simple gift.

"Eddie, your breakfast is ready," Janet Wagner called up the steps. "Come eat it while it's hot."

"Okay," I said. I picked up my box and looked around the hallway and the cot that had been my room for this stopping off place in my life. I wondered what kind of bed I would sleep in tonight. I started down the steps.

"Mom, look what Eddie gave me," Benjamin said with a wide smile.

"Hey, that's great. Eddie. That is so kind of you," Mrs. Wagner said.

The kids were all at the table in their places, but without their usual smiles and chatter.

"We feel bad you're leaving," Daniel said. "It's funny how the welfare doesn't even give you a warning. Aren't you scared?"

"This has happened to me before. Remember, I told you foster kids always have to move on? It's not fun not to know in advance, but maybe they think kids would worry if they did. Anyway, I don't have a choice."

"Here's a plate of eggs and bacon, Eddie," my foster mother said. "John, please pass the toast and jam down this way."

My queasy stomach was doing flip-flops like it always did when the unexpected was about to take place. I felt like I was going to have to jump off a high cliff into the fog. Who knows when I would eat my next meal, so I'd better eat no matter how I felt. I only hoped they wouldn't be sending Miss Westfield to move me to my next home. If only the welfare would send someone else this time.

"Eddie thanks for helping our family in so many ways when we have been going through hard times. I pray you will be happy and will adjust well in your new home," Janet Wagner said.

"I see a car coming up the driveway," John said as he looked out the window. "It's probably your ride."

Benjamin jumped up from the table still clutching his red, metal horse. He stood waiting for the knock at the door.

"Hello," he said as he opened the door wide. "Come in."

"Good morning, I'm Victor Hanson, a Social Worker for St. Croix County. I'm here to meet Eddie Brewster."

"That's me, sir," I said to this tall man with a dark brown cap and tan plaid jacket.

"Good to meet you, Eddie," Mr. Hanson said, as he reached out and shook my hand warmly.

"You folks have some snowy roads out this way," Mr. Hanson said in a kind voice. "My, what a fine looking family you have, Mrs. Wagner. Could I get you to sign this form, please?"

I took one last look at baby Julie, sleeping peacefully in her bassinet. She was so tiny. She was too small to be concerned about any of the Wagner family problems.

"Well then, I guess we'll be on our way, Eddie," Mr. Hanson said with a smile.

I put on my jacket and cap, picked up my cardboard box, and started to walk toward the door.

"Good bye Eddie," the children said in chorus.

"Yes, Eddie, good bye and we wish the very best for you," Janet Wagner said as she patted my shoulder. I noticed tears beginning to form in her eyes.

"Thank you. Goodbye everybody," I said, as I walked out the door.

"You can put your box in the back seat there and ride up front with me, if you wish," Mr. Hanson said.

"Good bye, Chip you good old dog. You've been a great friend," I said.

"You like dogs, do you?" Mr. Hanson asked.

"Yup, I sure do."

We started down the long driveway. For a moment, I looked back and saw the children and Janet Wagner waving on the porch. Then I turned and looked ahead to set my mind for what would happen next.

The End of *Book Two of—The Eddie Brewster Adventures*